# CORK STORIES

Edited by Madeleine D'Arcy & Laura McKenna

Doire Press

First published in 2024


Doire Press
Aille, Inverin
Co. Galway
www.doirepress.com


Layout: Lisa Frank
Cover design: Tríona Walsh
Cover image: Paulrommer SL @ shutterstock.com
Editor photos: Clare Keogh and Claire O'Rorke


Printed by Booksfactory
www.booksfactory.ie


Introduction copyright © Doire Press
Stories copyright © Their individual authors
Map copyright @ Tríona Walsh


ISBN 978-1-907682-99-5

We gratefully acknowledge the support and assistance of The Arts Council of Ireland / An Chomhairle Ealaíon.

# CONTENTS

# FOREWORD

Everyone in Cork has a story. Over the centuries, poets, biographers, novelists and short-story writers have honed their craft here and the contemporary writing scene in Cork today is flourishing. *Cork Stories* reflects the vibrant literary tradition and love for the city and its environs that has always existed.

In *Cork Stories*, Madeleine D'Arcy and Laura McKenna have assembled an amazing record of contemporary short fiction in Cork right now. This anthology showcases an array of new voices and well-established writers living in or connected to Cork.

These stories take us on a tour of Cork city and county which we see through the eyes of the writers and their characters. Cork humour, often dark, prevails on our journey.

We are led along by the river past the apartment of King Kong and Godzilla off Douglas Street, and up to Carmel's penthouse in the Elysian. We take a peek at Cork institutions, like the Imperial Hotel, Reidy's Wine Vaults and the Victoria Hospital where Protestant nurses kiss Catholic boys. From Buxton Hill, we see 'the palm of the city fill up with its lights'. Cork writers are a huge part of this illumination of the city.

As we travel outside the city, the stories take us to coastal towns like Ballycotton, Passage West and Kinsale, as well as to inland areas, such as Kanturk and Mallow. These stories shine a light on some of the darker corners of human existence. But all is not lost. We can outrun our sadness and join Pat, laughing and shouting, 'Run! Run, you beautiful bastards!' The collection firmly captures the spirit and personality of Cork and its people.

I am privileged to work with Cork-based writers and organisations through my role in Cork City Libraries. Congratulations to Doire Press for publishing this anthology and for their continued dedication to Irish writing.

Patricia Looney
Acting Cork City Librarian
5th December, 2023

# INTRODUCTION

The stories in this anthology are all set in Cork, the largest county in Ireland with the longest coastline and a great variety of landscapes, townscapes and seascapes. The characters inhabit such disparate settings as city streets, coastal towns like Ballycotton and Kinsale and townlands around Mallow and Kanturk. Two maps — one of the city and another of the county — are included in this book, so that you, the reader, can pinpoint the location of each story and walk in the footsteps of these fictional characters.

All of the stories have been written by authors who live in Cork or have a strong connection with the city or the county. We are delighted to include the work of acclaimed short story writers whose names are familiar to a wide readership. It has also been a pleasure to discover stories by writers who are, perhaps, less well-known at present, but whose work demonstrates an intuitive affinity for the form.

Humour looms large in many of the stories: the sly aside, the witty turn of phrase and an occasional laugh-out-loud moment. No Cork collection would be complete without a dash of Cork slang or vernacular, whether it be city or rural. If there is any unifying element across the anthology, it is the strong narrative voices that carry the stories, each one distinctive. While we were keen to focus on the contemporary, some stories are set in the past. A good short story is a good story regardless of its place in time.

But what exactly is a short story, you might ask? The short story is slippery. It defies generalisation. Kate Atkinson has said that 'the story is not the little sister of the novel'. Joyce Carol Oates has written that 'it represents a concentration of the imagination... and when it ends, the attentive reader understands why.' James Joyce spoke of epiphanies. Claire Keegan talks about 'yearning'. Frank O'Connor identified 'an intense awareness of human loneliness' at the heart of a short story, and that is true of many in this collection. The best short stories tend not to be showy or dramatic. They work on you in a subtle way, until, with a kind of quiet satisfaction, you see the world a little differently.

We have enjoyed bringing these stories together. We have entered the world of each story, line by line, word by word. We have realised — not for the first time — that it's not an easy feat to write a good short story. It involves not just inspiration, but also hard work, craft, humility and dedication. It takes time to get the words down right.

Is there such a thing as a typical Cork story? When an anthology is defined by a geographical boundary, it is tempting to look for some unifying element determined by place or some similarities of theme, idiom or outlook. These stories reflect the idiosyncratic relationship between the characters and their environment, whether that is the built and peopled space of the city or the open countryside and coastal areas.

To quote Alastair MacLeod, 'The best fiction is specific in its setting but universal in its theme.' And so it is with this anthology. The stories are all set in Cork, but the themes are universal. They present Cork in all its colour and character. No two stories are the same; each is unique, in and of itself. We hope that you enjoy them and that you will come to the same conclusion as we did. There is *no* typical Cork story.

Madeleine D'Arcy and Laura McKenna
Co-Editors

*Anne O'Leary*

# THE COOK AND THE STAR

The first time she sees the Hollywood star, he is cautiously descending the staircase. He has not noticed her standing in the kitchen doorway and his large body is tilted sideways as if he is negotiating a steep hillside. He is snorting with the effort, fingers gripping the banister. Halfway down, he spots her. Immediately, his wheezing stills and his back straightens.

'You must be my saviour,' he says. His famous, velvet voice is gentler than she expects. The cook will recall its melodious sound many times afterwards.

She is afraid to speak until he has completed his descent, terrified of the repercussions if he were to trip. She keeps smiling, trying not to stare yet committing every detail to memory.

When he reaches the bottom step, his foot tapping out solid ground, she says, 'It's such a pleasure to meet you.' She has an urge to curtsy.

'Why, the pleasure is all mine, my dear,' he says, with a wave of his hand. 'You are the keeper of the kitchen, therefore you are almighty. I bow before you.' He does a mock flourish that reveals sagging underarms.

Up close, he is a block of a man, seeming as wide as he is tall. A baseball cap throws his eyes into shade, but even so she can see the strain on his face.

'What would you like for breakfast? I can make anything that takes your fancy,' she says. She points him in the direction of the formal dining room, but he turns instead towards the kitchen.

'Whatever people normally eat in Ireland,' he says. 'I like to immerse myself in the local culture, so you must be my guide. But first, some coffee if I may.'

He takes a seat at the large kitchen table that overlooks the old stable yard. Outside, mist envelops everything. The high walls that shield the country house from prying eyes are invisible in the dim morning. It feels as if they're the only two people in the world.

Her hands are like an amateur's as she measures coffee for the espresso machine. From the enormous fridge, she takes out sausages, rashers and black pudding. He looks like a man who will do justice to a decent fry. While she works, he quizzes her. He is playing an Irish country doctor in the film and needs to work on his accent. 'Me accent,' he says. He would love to practise it with her.

'Oh, fire away,' she says, thinking how incredible it is that she should be helping an actual Hollywood star with his research. She imagines the looks on people's faces if she were to tell them. The mere thought of it is a tonic.

'Fire away,' he repeats, with a lilt that is more Brooklyn than Cork.

He asks peculiar questions, like whether she has ever been out of the town.

'Well, I went to visit my brother and his wife in Hoboken, New Jersey once,' she says. 'I still have my Macy's carrier bags from New York. They're great for my library books.'

She has questions she would like to ask him, but holds her tongue because she has been instructed not to overstep the mark. It comes as a surprise that he is willing to talk, and she has to keep reminding herself that she must remain professional. She knows a fair bit about his personal life — everyone does, especially the recent events — but all of it is off limits.

She asks what his first impressions are of Ireland.

'It's beautiful, so mystical,' he says, gazing out the window at what is now settling into a dirty drizzle. 'I have wanted to come here all my life. My mother was Irish, you know.'

She does know. She's seen TV interviews in which he talked about his mother, and knows the woman was a raging alcoholic and how, as a youngster, he had the task of carting her home drunk from bars. It reminded her of her husband, who also needed encouragement in that area.

When he has finished breakfast, folding slice after slice of butter-dripping toast into his mouth, he thanks her with the manners of a Victorian gentleman and goes to get ready. The sound of him inching back up the stairs fills her with fear until he's safely on the landing. His driver arrives on the dot of eight, and the star says he will have someone call as soon as they know when they will wrap for the day.

'I'll have your dinner ready for you,' she says, filing away the phrase 'wrap for the day' for future reference.

She loads the dishwasher, resisting the mad notion to put the cup that touched his lips into her bag as a keepsake.

Afterwards, she drives into town to pick up sirloin from the good butcher.

When he returns in the evening, he is grey with fatigue and requests dinner on a tray. He eats two large steaks and three desserts while watching RTE news in the living room. From the hallway, she hears him repeating certain words over and over. 'Thirty. Tirty. Turtee...'

Other than thanking her for a fine meal, he says little and tells her she is free to go once she's served his coffee. As she is leaving, he casually asks where the drinks cabinet is kept.

'Oh, there is none,' she says.

It's pure awkward, but he doesn't seem surprised. He repeats, 'None,' but makes it sound like 'non'.

His eyes search the room anyway. She does not tell him that the cabinet has been removed on instruction.

Once home, she makes beans on toast and eats it in bed. She sets the alarm for six, but keeps waking to check it throughout the night.

Every morning of that first week follows the same pattern. The star follows the smell of sausages sizzling in the pan and sits in the kitchen while she works. He asks if she has a family, whether she is a local, whether she enjoys living here. She tells him that the brother in Hoboken passed away, but she has a daughter travelling in the Far East and an ex-husband about whom the less said the better. She says she has lived here all her life and can't imagine living anywhere else.

'Though I've a yen to visit places like California now alright,' she adds on the fifth morning, by which time she is feeling surprisingly at ease.

'It is very beautiful,' he agrees. 'I am fortunate to have a house overlooking the ocean. I chose it because it felt like a haven. And nothing beats the purity of that sea air.'

His script rests against a fruit bowl so he can study his lines as he eats. From her angle at the cooker, she observes a thinning at the top of his head and realises that the hair unsuccessfully combed across it is dyed a shade too dark for his freckled scalp. She remembers a time when he was so handsome women screamed at the sight of him. His posters hung in every young girl's bedroom, her own included. She hopes his hair and make-up people think to tuck away the bald patch before allowing him in front of the cameras — she doesn't like to think of his vulnerability on show in a multiplex.

There is little to do during the day, but she doesn't mind as there's nowhere else for her to be. Occasionally, she makes tea for the cleaner who comes in twice a week, but she finds the woman a shocking gossip.

'You should see his room,' the cleaner whispers, though there is no one nearby. 'The dresser is covered with prescription bottles. It's like a chemist's up there. And he's got photos of the son *everywhere*. It's creepy. Seriously, go and have a peep. I won't tell anyone.'

The cook says she had better get started on the roast lamb. As she spikes it with fragrant rosemary from the garden, she wonders what it must be like to have every aspect of your life on show. Imagine people poking around her own bedroom? How they would smirk at the stack of romance novels from the library, the cheap trinkets in the souvenir bowl, the single picture of herself and her daughter at the beach, holding ice creams and actually smiling.

She can't remember a time when she's felt happier. It isn't just the money, though that in itself is a godsend. It won't come anywhere near to covering the debts her husband has left in his wake, but it will at least allow her to show her face in a few places that had become an embarrassment. Her boss is paying well beyond the going rate but has stressed it's largely for her to keep her mouth shut. He has warned that strangers might approach her — journalists angling for information. She is to ignore them, play dumb.

'That won't come too hard, will it?' he'd joked, so like her husband that for an instant it felt like a slap.

The first time is when she's buying doughnuts in the bakery because the star has a hankering. A woman stands close to her at the counter and strikes up a conversation. It's casual to begin with, so the cook doesn't realise what is happening until the woman mentions how exciting it is to have a film set on their doorstep. The cook has foolishly blurted out that she is involved in the production when she sees something in the woman's face. An exaggerated look of surprise as she breathes, 'Really?' that tells the cook the woman already knows this. She removes herself from the conversation as politely as she can — plays dumb with ease.

The second time it is a man. He hands her his business card as she's putting shopping bags in the boot of her Toyota Starlet.

'I'd love to talk to you, and we pay well,' he says, sharp eyes taking in the baldness of her tyres. 'Your name won't be mentioned.'

The star seems wearier with every passing day. He leaves early — his driver outside the door at dawn some mornings — and returns after eight every evening when they lose the good light. He carries his script about the house at all times. It flutters with Post-its, the curling pages a mess of highlighted passages and heavy notes in the margins. He mutters lines under his breath like a prayer, swearing if he goes wrong. When this happens, he apologises as if she is a fine lady unused to such vulgarity. If only he knew the filthy language her daughter used to come out with, rampaging through their house like a demon whenever she was wrong with the world. The cook reckons Chrissy could have given the star a run for his money; you wouldn't hear the like of it in those gangster films that made his name. Things were bad even before the girl started going out God knows where with God knows who, vanishing for days on end doing God knows what.

Other than being on set, the star doesn't leave the house. The rest of the cast have taken up residence at the big spa resort with the serenity pool, so the star opting for an old house in the middle of nowhere is a source of press speculation. But the feeling around the area is that it's hardly surprising he wants to be left alone when he is still in mourning, and isn't he fantastic to be working at all under the circumstances?

Most days the sets, using picturesque corners of the town, are encircled by curious onlookers. The cook sees them on her shopping trips, sitting on walls with good vantage points: gangs of teenagers, entire families, lone pensioners with flasks of tea. They watch as lighting rigs are set up and crew members with walkie-talkies and American accents stride around importantly. So many visitors are drawn to the town for a glimpse of the star that the local businesses hang photos of him in their establishments. They're mostly of him in his younger days, when it was impossible to imagine him as anything other than perfect.

On the ninth day, the director, the handsome young co-star and the beautiful leading lady come to the house for dinner. Although the cook generally enjoys catering for groups, on this occasion it feels like an invasion. The smell of expensive aftershave and overpowering perfume fills the hallway. She hears them laughing in the dining room, their actorly voices ringing loud and false through the normally empty rooms. In the absence of alcohol, the evening ends early, and then the star comes to the kitchen. She is dead on her feet and waiting for permission to go home to her supper in bed. She might have a fried egg sandwich; that will be nice and quick.

'Thank God that's done,' he says. 'It's hard to suffer these gatherings sober. I feel I have to be someone I'm not. And I'm not even getting paid for my skills.'

'Still, the bit of company must be nice? Having a few friends around?'

'It's been a long time since I've had friends. These people talk about nothing of consequence,' he says. He compliments her Baileys cheesecake and helps himself to another piece.


On the tenth day, the star does not come down for breakfast. His car waits outside for almost an hour, until eventually the driver rings the bell.

'You'd better go knock on his bedroom door,' he says.

'Are you mad? I can't be doing that,' she says.

They hover in the hallway while the driver calls the executive producer. He says he'll handle it, and seconds later, they hear a mobile ringtone from the star's room directly above their heads. It rings out, unanswered.

The producer arrives soon afterwards, screeching up the driveway in a sports car that is slung low to the ground. He is a blur of suntan and gleaming cufflinks as he dashes past them up the stairs. She waits with the driver, who keeps asking, 'Will I call the ambulance? Do you think I should call the ambulance?' He seems more excited than worried, and has started taking photos on his phone of the hallway, the staircase, her staring up it.

Eventually, the producer comes down the stairs, talking on his mobile.

'Not possible, no. We'll revisit the situation tomorrow. No, the depression thing, I guess. I'll have him checked over. Well, you'll just have to rework it, I'm afraid...'

By the twelfth day, the star still hasn't materialised. When he wants food, he rings down to the kitchen, his voice a polite monotone. She leaves large trays outside his door and collects them afterwards, to find every plate scraped clean.

The producer comes around mornings and evenings, accompanied by doctors or the frantic director. Sometimes there is shouting from the star's bedroom. She is quizzed about what he eats and what he drinks. Does anyone come to the house? Does anyone call the landline?

'No, not a soul,' she says.

The newspapers report that the star has gone into hiding, despite everyone knowing very well where he is. Reporters camp out under sun umbrellas beside the gates to the property, occasionally buzzing the intercom for a statement. More than once, she spots the glint of a photographer up a tree with a camera.

Filming is suspended and the town's traders are worried the film will not now be finished. If it doesn't get made, the tourists won't flock to see the locations. Fair enough he's lost a son to a tragic overdose, they say, but he is contractually obliged. And it isn't as if he was much of a father while the boy was alive, off having affairs with starlets and whatnot. Surely to God for millions of dollars the man could drag himself out of bed and do a bit of acting? How hard could it be? Sources close to the star say he's difficult, he's back on the booze, back on the drugs. People who have never before shown the slightest interest in her existence now stop her on the street to ask what's the story with himself? And she says sure she's only the cook, what would she know?

On the fifteenth day, a Monday, the star appears in the kitchen at the usual time. His skin looks as if it hasn't been touched by sunlight for years, his eyes are ringed with brown shadows. An orange-coloured Aran jumper strains across his middle.

'I wonder if I may trouble you to rustle up some breakfast?' he asks, his voice little more than a whisper.

She debates whether she should speak or stay quiet as she turns sausages in the pan, chops mushrooms, lays bacon out in neat lines.

'I need to get away from here,' he says to her back.

'Will I call your driver, sir? I'm sure he could be here quite quickly.'

'I was hoping you might take me.'

'Me?' she says, trying to picture him in her clapped-out car. 'Take you where?'

'I don't care. Anywhere. I just need out.'

She hesitates so long that he offers to reimburse her for her time.

'Oh, it's not that, sir. I'm just not accustomed to ferrying celebrities around in my old jalopy.'

'Then I'd be honoured to be the first,' he says.

She doesn't dare refuse him, yet she wonders what the executive producer and director, and indeed her boss, will say. But it isn't as if the star is being held prisoner, is it?

He looks utterly wrong in the Starlet, his bulk spilling out in every direction like dough that has been left to rise for too long. He's wearing his baseball cap, a pair of sunglasses and a large scarf with a skull pattern covering the bottom half of his face. The paparazzi at the entrance don't realise it's him in the passenger seat until the last minute, so they only get a few shots before she floors it through the electronic gates and down the road. Checking her rear-view mirror as characters in heist movies do, she is pleased to see that none of them has been quick enough to follow in pursuit.

She drives without knowing where she's heading. Peace, she thinks. He needs somewhere peaceful. She tries to remember the last time she felt peaceful and where that might have been. Suddenly, she knows.

It's a short drive along winding country roads, the air fresh with the smell of cut grass. Summer hedge growth caresses the car on the tighter bends, which makes him jittery. He asks if she knows any good pubs.

'No, no pubs where we're going,' she says.

It probably doesn't look as exotic as the view he's used to from his glamorous Californian windows, but it will hopefully work its magic. He glances about as she manoeuvres around potholes in the small car park and pulls up facing the beach. It is deserted except for the odd dog walker and a couple of swimmers in wetsuits.

'What do we do now?' he asks.

'I thought you might like an ice cream,' she replies.

'An ice cream?'

'Yes, the van over there sells the finest ice cream cones in all of Ireland.'

She points at a shabby ice cream van by the car park entrance, manned by a sulky teen. The lad doesn't even glance at them as he takes two cones, swirls the soft ice cream to perfect peaks, then jabs a Flake into each. The star stands next to her, for all the world like *The Invisible Man* with his face covered by the baseball cap, glasses and scarf.

He removes the scarf when they are safely sitting on the low wall that curves down to the beach, away from possible cameras. Not that there's much likelihood of them lurking in this empty place.

They eat their ice creams, watching the waves.

'What is that island out there?' he asks. On the horizon, the lighthouse rises like a castle in a fairy tale, a pathway carving a zig-zag up through the rocks from the landing pier.

'That's Ballycotton lighthouse. Isn't it like a child's drawing? My daughter used to dream of living in it.'

'A beautiful place. But desolate.'

'I wouldn't fancy going for my weekly shop in the winter, that's for sure.'

Seagulls swoop over the calm waters, crying to each other. There's a soft hiss and rake of the waves as they slowly claim the beach. The taste of sea salt in the air mingles with the vanilla of the ice cream.

'This is pleasant,' he says.

'It never fails to cheer me up,' she replies. 'There's something about the sea that makes you feel small, but not in a bad way. More like we're all the same, just part of this big mad world, getting by.'

'Perhaps that's why I also feel drawn to it.'

'A famous person like you could never feel small, surely?'

'I feel small all the time. And bad. I'm a bad man, a fake. I even fake professionally, get paid big bucks for it, as you know.'

His accent has lost that odd lilt he's been practising. The sunglasses shield his eyes, but she knows the lost look they hold.

'You shouldn't be so hard on yourself. Sure aren't you doing your best?'

He takes a large bite of the Flake, eating half of it in one mouthful. 'You know, I keep asking myself that? And the truth is, most of the time I don't have to try. I do what I want and leave others to mop up after me. I make a bare-minimum effort and people are satisfied because my name sells. But I'm a flop at the things that really matter. Being a good husband, a good father.'

'There's no training for being a parent. Really, there should be courses you could take, we're all hopeless.'

'Your daughter,' he says. 'Do you see her often?'

'It's been a while,' the cook admits.

He nods and kindly doesn't ask any more.

Down at the shoreline, two women pause to take off their shoes and socks and start paddling carefully, shrieking at the still chilly water. They look alike, possibly mother and daughter.

'Actually, she's never coming back.'

There. She has said it. She's never said it before. There's been no one to tell, no one who would truly care to know.

'What?' the star asks. He is using his scarf to dab at a dribble of ice cream on his unshaven chin.

'My daughter. Chrissy. I don't think she's ever coming back. I let her down very badly, didn't stick up for her when I should have. My husband was not an easy man to live with.'

'I'm sure you tried,' he says.

'I didn't do enough. But you know yourself—it's bad when you have time to think of all the ways you should have done things. I'd go pure mad if I stopped long enough for that. Keep working is the only way.'

He nods and points the remainder of his ice cream cone towards the horizon. 'Hopefully your daughter is out there living a blessed life in the Far East.'

Hopefully she is living a blessed life. Hopefully she is still living. The cook can't imagine how he is coping with the loss of his son, and with the press writing articles about how fame damages celebrities' children. What has fame to do with it? One day, when the cleaner wasn't about, she gave in and peeped into his bedroom. There on his locker were photos of his boy, so young and so beautiful. She thinks of the photo of herself and Chrissy in her own room, her daughter aged eleven, still happy to sit on a wall by the sea and enjoy an ice cream together. That's the last time she can recall seeing the girl happy. She glances at the star and wants to say something, but there's nothing to say. She knows it is best not to dwell on these things, just enjoy the moment for what it is.

'This is very pleasant,' the star says again, and takes the deepest of breaths. 'That sea air. So cleansing.' He smiles, and behind the sunglasses she sees the ghost of laughter lines.

'It is,' she agrees.

It's what she hoped for, a moment's respite, with gentle sun on her face and a Hollywood star beside her who was once the handsomest man alive.

*Tadhg Coakley*

# A PURE DOTE

Later, Nuala would wonder why it was always the bloody keys that Gerry kept losing. They ended up being found in the usual places — pockets or door-locks or the ignition. At first, she hadn't taken much notice of it; he was busy, they were all busy. So what if he'd become a bit forgetful, even at forty?

One evening, when he was going to a meeting up in the Mallow GAA complex, she saw him in the hall staring at the keys as if he didn't know what they were or what to do with them. It was then that alarm bells started ringing. She knew they were in big trouble on their way to Mrs O'Connell's funeral that wet Friday night in October. When he was driving through Buttevant and he asked her where they were going.

Oliver, the GP, was matter-of-fact.

'It isn't looking good, guys,' he said, and she had always hated that word 'guys' and the way people used it. People aren't 'guys'; she isn't a 'guy'. 'Don't call me a "guy", you asshole,' she wanted to shout in his face but, of course, she said nothing.

'But you never know. There could be a simple cause and if there is, the neurologist will find it,' he said, and he washed his hands of it. They never went back to him. What a cold fish for a doctor, a horrible man, and she doesn't say that often.

*Neurologist.* The word alone is frightening, drawing up an image of a brain in a dish. But Nuala realised quickly that fear was a luxury she could not afford, so she didn't countenance it. Whatever about feeling it from time to time, he would never see it in her eyes, she decided — and he never did, never will.

Oliver had not used the words, but the neurologist (a kindlier man than the GP, she had to admit — he had seemed sorry for what he was telling them) didn't hesitate in that cold office beside CUH.

Early onset dementia. Early. Onset. Dementia.

And that was that.

'Sticks and stones may break my bones but words will never hurt me?' Try telling that to someone diagnosed with early onset dementia in the prime of his life, with a wife and three young kids and a mortgage. Try telling it to his wife and children, his friends and family. Then you'll know what hurt is. Nuala knew what hurt was. Hurt was the love of your life turning into a helpless child, so that you have to look after him every day and sleep beside him every night and feed him and wash him and change his nappies day-in, day-out — the fine man you gave your heart and soul and body to — now a statue, a nothing, a mockery. Hurt was watching your children grow up without a father, but having to care for a shadow of a man who should be caring for them. Hurt was having to fight and fight and fight with strangers, day-in and day-out, for every entitlement, every support, waiting on phone lines, standing in queues, filling out online forms, swallowing the shame of the hand-outs she never in her life expected that she would be forced to accept. She would take the sticks and stones any day.

Oh, Gerry was brave, he was her brave man. His first fear was Huntington's and Pick's because they were hereditary and he was thinking about the children. When he had all those tests done and they were negative, he drew breath.

'I might be lucky,' he said one night in front of the fire. 'I might not have given it to them.'

She smiled. She hadn't felt lucky in a long time, but she knew she was and always would be. She took his hand and said, 'We'll face it together, all the way, boy.'

She sang a verse of that Johnny Cash song he liked, and he joined in. Later, they went upstairs and made love. In hindsight, she knew that was the night Jack was conceived, as sure as God. Sometimes you just know. Madness, of course, to have Jack when they did, but she wouldn't send him back and he the image of his lovely father.

The descent was rapid and spectacular, if that's the right word — she didn't even think about it anymore, what was the point? After that it had been sadness after sadness: the last day at work, the last time he drove, the last time they made love, the last day he fed himself, the last match he went to, the last time he spoke, the last time he laughed, the last time he went out, the last time he acknowledged her, the last time he smiled. Now there are no more lasts, are there? And won't be, until the last last.

The last time he smiled was the worst because it was the final expression he ever showed. Now he was trapped in there somewhere, thinking something, feeling something — nobody knew what, nobody could tell them. To herself, she called it his 'white room'. She imagined him in a room full of white light, so bright that there was nothing else visible — no walls, no ceiling, not even a floor. It didn't hurt, there was no distress, there was no past, no future, no other people — nothing but the pure white light. She didn't know where she got the idea from, a film maybe.

They used to have a joke and it was to that joke that he gave her his last few smiles. It was a dirty joke, she could only tell him when they were alone, when the kids were gone to bed. One night she wanted a smile out of him so she sat down and told him, as usual:

*Two deaf people get married. After several nights of fumbling around and misunderstandings in bed in the dark, the wife decides to find a way for them to communicate. 'Honey,' she signs, 'why don't we agree on some simple signals? So, at night, if you want to have sex with me, reach over and squeeze my left breast once. If you don't want to have sex, reach over and squeeze my right breast once.' The husband thinks this is a great idea and signs back to his wife, 'Great idea, so if YOU want to have sex with ME, reach over and pull on my penis once. If you don't want to have sex, reach over and pull on my penis... fifty times!'*

She finished the joke with a flourish, but there was no smile. Gerry just looked at the television, looked at her and then turned back to the television. Nothing.

Nothing is the worst; there are no words for nothing.

It was hard on the kids too, though Caoimhe and Jack

escaped the full brunt of it, being so young — to them, in a way, their father was like an old beloved family pet with whom they had to be patient and speak to now and again and kiss goodnight. Nuala had seen Caoimhe grow tired of that role lately, and she would have to say something to her before long.

It was hardest on William, she knew that. At eighteen, he was old enough to remember his father in his prime and all the things they used to do together. Aisling, her eldest, her rock, was a pleaser and just wanted to help as often and as much as she could. She missed her daddy, that was for sure, but shaving him or feeding him brought her close to him and she felt better for having done him some good. For William, those acts were abominable, unnatural, and he hated the idea of them and he hated doing them and then he hated himself for his feelings. The resentment grew and grew until he broke down one night at Christmas the year before last, when she had him to herself, and she drew it out of him and he let it all go.

'It's not fair, it's not fair, I hate it,' he cried, wiping his eyes, sitting in the seat Nuala always associated with Gerry.

'It isn't, love. Not to your dad, not to me, not to you or Aisling, or Caoimhe or Jack. Or his own mother, poor Cassie,' she said. 'You know what, William, it's fucking shit.'

The shock drew him out of his misery and he laughed. So did she.

'Now,' she said, glancing at the clock. 'Go out to the fridge and get a can for yourself and get the bottle of Baileys and a glass out of the press. We'll have a Christmas drink, just you and me. Not a word to the others.'

On that September Sunday, after Mass in The Church of The Resurrection, she sat down in front of Gerry, but just to the side so he could still see the television. The All-Ireland was coming on and Cork were playing. He watched sports for hours at a time, thanks be to God, not that anybody knew how much he could take in.

She combed her fingers though his hair, his lovely sandy-coloured hair that she loved to keep tidy with the sharp scissors she hid in the press and wouldn't let anybody else use. He watched the television. She looked into his eyes; was there movement there? She could never tell, but she was convinced he still knew her.

She smiled at him and kissed his cheek. Nobody took a blind bit of notice of her, they were all used to her by now. They had a crowd in the room, settling down for the match.

'Will we win, Gerry? I think we will,' she said. 'Up the Rebels!'

She thought about all the matches they had attended together in the early days, when they had just begun going out. Lord God, how her quiet man used to shout and roar at the Mallow hurlers and the referee. Then he'd be all apologies to her afterwards. Sure she didn't care, as long as she was with him — he never said a cross word to her.

An hour later, while she was washing up in the kitchen, William came in looking crestfallen.

'What's up, love, are we losing?'

'Yes, and we've run out of beer.'

'Why don't you pop down to Dano's and get some more?'

'I've had three cans, Mam, and I don't want to miss the end of the match.'

'Okay, love, I'll go down,' she said and took off her apron.

On the way home, she pulled into St Anthony's Terrace, where she had grown up. It looked tatty. Rubbish bins over-flowed outside Brennans' and Dolans', and their front gardens were a disgrace. She parked at number twenty-one, her family's old house, where she had first made love to Gerry when she was seventeen and her parents had gone away for the weekend to Killarney. He thought he was the whole man after that, and she thought she was a full-grown woman too. There was no going back after that — for both of them. It was 1986, the summer of 'Lady in Red', and they used to dance to it every Friday night in the Hi-B disco, their bodies moulded into each other's, French kissing.

She closed her eyes and listened — she could hear the song so clearly.

She pressed her head back against the headrest and felt the pain severing her in two.

'Oh, God,' she said, in a whimper. 'Oh, God.'

She wrenched at the steering wheel and squeezed it and pulled it until her arms hurt. She growled through clenched teeth and shouted: 'Fuck, fuck, fuck, fuck, fuck,' until something bubbled up inside her, making her dizzy and sick. She banged her head against the headrest and it felt good so she did it again, swinging back with more force each time, the thumping sound satisfying her, the pain in her neck satisfying her.

Later, weak and watery, she turned the bend into the Cork Road for home. She hummed the little moon lullaby her mother used to sing her as a child. *I see the moon, the moon sees me.* Her lovely mam. God, she was a pure dote.

'Every day is a miracle,' her dad used to say. Every day is a miracle.

As she approached the house and was about to pull in, Caoimhe jumped out onto the road, almost on top of the bonnet.

Nuala slammed on the brakes and Caoimhe, red-faced, ran around to her door. She lowered the window to admonish the child but Caoimhe shouted: 'Dad's smiling, Dad's smiling, Mam. Come in, come in.'

When she got out of the car, Jack ran to her. 'Dad's smiling, Dad's smiling. Cork won and Dad's smiling.'

She took his hand and walked through. Of the nine people in the room, Gerry alone was watching the television — all the others were looking at her or at him. Aisling was crying and William, Nuala could see, was just about keeping it in check.

And there, on her brown-eyed handsome man's face, was a blissful smile; not just in his lips but in his cheeks and his eyes and his forehead. The joy streamed out of her Gerry, taking years off him. Bringing him back to them.

She gasped and knelt beside him. 'Oh, Gerry,' she said, and he turned his face to her, the smile never wavering, and he saw her. He saw her. Then he turned back to the television, which showed grinning young men in red jerseys parade a cup around a huge stadium.

Caoimhe pulled at the sleeve of her blouse. 'Mam? Mam?' she said, pulling.

Nuala, unmoving, said: 'Yes, love?'

'Will Daddy get better now? Now that Cork won?'

Jolted, Nuala turned to her. 'Oh, no, love, no he won't get better, but isn't it lovely to see him smile again?'

She moved Jack and Caoimhe in front of her, put her arms around them and pressed the side of her face into Caoimhe's hair. Together they watched Gerry smiling.

*Danny Denton*

# A LOVE LETTER IN THE MIDSUMMER

That midsummer she wrote him a love letter from Leenane. But it was not exactly a love letter, more a sort of teleplay about King Kong and Godzilla sharing an apartment off Douglas Street, long after their various escapades in Japan and New York and across the world's oceans. He'd kept the letter in his back pocket all evening, and when at last the pub was swept clean and wiped down and locked up, he walked along by Sullivan's Quay and stopped on a riverside bench there. Taking out the letter, he felt that heavy compression of expectation in his chest. He turned the scuffed white envelope over in his hand and then watched the black river purling away towards the College of Comm. A few stragglers lingered on the opposite boardwalk, delaying the inevitable. It was a balmy July night. With a long exhalation of sweet worry, he opened the letter.

Morning in the apartment. King Kong poked his dishevelled head out of the bedroom doorframe, taking in the scope of the kitchen and living area.

'You cleaned up,' Kong said. 'Sorry.'

Godzilla sat at the table, browsing away on his laptop, his cup of tea to one side. 'You're grand,' he consoled, not for the first time.

Kong crossed to the kitchen on shaky legs and began the ritual of going through the cupboards, hanging out of them and grumbling, looking perhaps for something that wasn't there.

'How bad was it?' he eventually asked.

'You owe me a pint.' Godzilla's claw deftly scrolled and clacked — Google searches no doubt. 'Red wine and broken glass all over the floor.'

Kong crumpled. 'Oh Jesus. Sorry.'

It was a small apartment, each of their rooms tight doubles, the kitchen-living area dark and compact, but they counter-acted this by keeping the place relatively tidy and more or less free of mementos or trinkets. For obvious reasons, they hadn't kept much from the old days; they just wanted to see out middle age with a modicum of dignity and anonymity. Which was difficult given Kong's indoor drinking and Godzilla's constant struggle to cover his rent. Kong settled at the table now with some BananaBix and yesterday's crumpled paper.

'Thanks for cleaning up after me, man. I'll make it up to you.'

Godzilla raised a claw-thumb while his beady eyes roamed the screen; the laptop engine revved with the effort of it all.

'How's the job hunt going?' Kong asked.

'Not much out there. Menial jobs, minimum wage jobs, but I'm too long in the tooth now to be going back to all that.'

Kong thought it was a bit rich to be looking down on jobs when a fella had nothing, but he wouldn't make the mistake of saying that again. They were still re-building Turner's Cross after that last drunken argument. So instead he said in solidarity: 'Something will come up eventually.'

'Yea,' Godzilla agreed. But then he said: 'It's amazing. It doesn't seem fair that a fella can make an effort his whole life and yet end up in his fifties stressing out about covering the rent.'

'Yea.' Kong felt it coming now and buried his head in his cereal.

'It doesn't seem fair, does it? Like, I'm not a mess. I don't have addiction issues; I never messed anyone about. I'm not lazy or stupid. All I ever did those times was defend myself, and other than that I worked hard my whole life. And now here I am on the dole at fifty-three and — no offence — sharing a gaff with a giant gorilla with a penchant for classic movies and smashing the place up of a Tuesday. No offence.'

'None taken.'

Actually, they were a good team. Godzilla did most of the cleaning and knew when the bins went out, while Kong was the better cook, the better company, and had those big loving eyes when it came to plamásing people. Not to mention that he covered more than his share of the rent and bills, more often than not, and never asked for it back.

'It's amazing how life passes you by,' Godzilla said. 'How you just keep on moving. Reacting. Making decisions on the hoof for years on end without ever really taking stock. Never looking around and figuring out who you actually are. Like, mentally, I still feel twenty-two. Like I'm still on the cusp of figuring myself out. D'you know what I mean? Like, how did I even become whatever it is that I am now? Who even am I? A fucking nuclear explosion is what I am, and all the rest is contamination. Recovering ground. Scurrying to keep up. How does anyone even go about becoming the person they wanted to become? How does that happen?'

He was all aglow, there at the kitchen table, the laptop prone between his scaly elbows. 'What do you think?' he asked Kong.

Kong thought about it, or pretended to. 'I dunno. I think you're in a shitty situation. But something will come along.' He thought better of saying he'd ask around the site for work. 'What about re-training? You'd make a great teacher, you know? You're organised, intelligent, and yet you've *lived*.'

Godzilla raised his eyes to the ceiling and sighed. The glow cooled. 'I miss the old days... The gallavanting.'

'Yea. You and me both.'

'What about you? Do *you* have regrets?'

And funnily enough, as Kong pretended to reminisce he did reminisce. And things came flooding. 'Yea, I do. Loads in fact.'

'Like what?'

'... I regret not finding a way to deal with myself earlier. To listen to myself. I regret taking things too seriously. I regret not reaching out to people earlier. I wish I'd done CBT twenty years before I actually did...'

'But that wasn't your fault. You were on your own. We both were.'

'Yea, but do you ever think about how many people we hurt over the years?'

'But we were fighting for our lives?'

'Yea but still. A lot of regrets.'

'Are you thinking about her?'

'Well, yea. But it's not that simple. Not just her. A lot of people. I did damage.'

'We both did.'

'And here we are.'

'Here we are, taking stock.' Godzilla closed the laptop down. 'The funny thing about it is that you grow up thinking about who you'll become. *When I'm older...* All that. But you never get beyond planning mode. Even now I still feel like I'm growing up. I'm copy-pasting CVs there and I'm thinking in the future-conditional tense. I'll be doing that on my deathbed.'

'Yea,' Kong said. 'And yet you've been someone for fifty-three years. And me for forty-eight.'

'Yea... That's mad isn't it?'

'It is.'

Godzilla leaned back, stretched. 'You headed to work?'

'I better do a bit I suppose.'

'Mind if I walk in with you? I could do with a stroll along the quays...'

The letter ended there, with a kiss, and this man found himself on Sullivan's Quay again, thinking: how in the name of God was that a love letter? She had specifically said in the text message that she'd posted him 'a love letter'. Was this it? Well what was the message? Did she have regrets? Had he done something wrong and this was an elaborate way of breaking it off? Or was it a reference to some conversation they'd had, some morning after? Would he see her again this summer? Or ever?

He folded the letter up and this time put it in his shirt pocket, over his heart. Over by the boardwalk they were settling down for the night, and he realised they were not lingering but homeless. He stood to go. It was true that he lived near Douglas Street. And that he was fifty-three and she forty-eight. They were two things in common with the teleplay. But he loved his job. And she would find something, surely, if she moved to Cork for good.

He remembered again, as he walked the dark-windowed streets, her blatant, giddy arrival into the pub that first night.

'You're old for a barman,' she'd grinned. 'Not like the usual shiny college kids.'

'I'm a career man,' he'd answered casually.

That was a summer night too, long ago now it felt.

'Like the French waiters,' she said.

'Exactly,' he said. 'I'm a refined individual.'

'My friend,' she said. 'We are *all* refined individuals.'

*Gráinne Murphy*

# NOTHING SURER

He kept his father's old Stanley hammer under the bed. Insurance, he thought, against a growing list of bothers. Next door's dog barking at something in the night. A light moving where it shouldn't. The world gone to holy hell and himself weakening by the new time.

Still, if time was a curse, routine was the cure. Today just a day like any other. The ball of the hammer was solid against his heel when he sat on the edge of the bed. Shoes on, face the world. Ellen would phone in the afternoon, she'd said.

At midday, he snapped on the old Philips radio in the kitchen, turning it up so loud it could be heard by anyone poking around the yard. *Vary your routine*, Ellen kept telling him, but she had no need to worry: when he was at home, he had the Stanley; when he was out, he had the Philips. Two good wingmen.

He gathered his things — coat from the rack, cap from the hook, key from the dresser drawer — and set off for the hotel and a hot dinner. Left to his own devices, Áine used to say, he would sit a hunk of buttery bread under a slice of ham at eight o'clock, twelve-thirty, six o'clock. That time she was away in hospital on women's business, himself and Ellen nearly lived on sandwiches. It didn't do them any harm except the once, when Ellen's front tooth came out in the crust and he had only a tenner to leave under her pillow for the fairy. An expensive lesson at the time, but they laughed about it for long years after.

He crossed the back yard and went out into the narrow alley that ran the length of the nine houses before meeting Cork Street at the far end. When they were all young and new to the terrace, there was talk of pushing everyone's backyard out a metre instead. Making room enough for a decent-sized workshop for the men with tools, or a shed to hold coal and deckchairs for the rest of them. Then babies crept along the row one-by-one and the insides of houses had more pressing needs.

Town was quiet now the tourists were gone and it was an ease to walk the footpath with his two hands swinging. Along Pearse Street, the shops were all decked out for Halloween. Mylie Murphy's had some kind of arty grey cobwebbing draped across the bicycles and fishing poles in the window. It took him back. He might have been looking in the door of his father's neglected garden shed, towards the end. His father's twisted hands and shook voice — *take something, won't you* — and himself taking the hammer amid a stream of rawmeish about how handy it would be. Anything to stop his father talking.

The pumpkin at the front of the display wouldn't last the week until Halloween if he was any judge. The pumpkin on their own front step used to be his department. Driving up to the city to the English Market with Ellen to pick out a likely specimen, then home again, debating who they might model it on. He was particularly proud of the E.T. year. There wasn't much to it only two big holes with golf balls inside them for the googly eyes and a few wavy lines carved over them for the wrinkles. It was the addition of Ellen's old red cardigan with the hood that brought the whole thing together. It was worth the hour in the attic, poking through boxes of baby clothes and keepsakes, while Áine held the bottom of the ladder steady and swore blind she knew she'd kept that cardigan somewhere. Oh it was well worth it. They were the talk of the terrace that year.

On the night itself, he would let Ellen coax him into taking her out along the terrace and then into the streets further afield, her pillowcase held tight in one hand and then, as it filled up, in her two hands, and then eventually under his own oxter for the return home. There, they would find Áine still passing out the fun-size KitKats and Twixes, her hair caught up in a black hairband with a velvet spider swaying on top and her face bright with fun. *We had a lovely time*, he would pretend-grumble, *swapping sweets with the neighbours.*

At his time of life, Halloween was only a racket. This year, it would be lights off and the television on low and let them move on to next door.

He turned away from the window and walked up to the pedestrian crossing. There was a bit more pinch in the air today. He should get his gloves out of the wardrobe in the spare room and put them into his coat pockets, the way winter wouldn't catch him off-guard.

In the hotel bar, his table was waiting for him. A good view of
the harbour and all its goings on, but without feeling he was
on display. It was his table even in the height of the season.
The staff here knew which side their bread was buttered—seven
days of carvery, seven coffees, desserts on Saturday and Sunday,
times fifty-two. It added up.

He overheard Bea Doyle and Kitty Hennessy discussing it
in the porch of the church one Sunday, in that carrying half-
whisper that believed itself discreet.

'He'll head up now shortly for his roast dinner,' said Bea
Doyle.

'Perched above in the hotel, day in, day out. That must be
a fine pension,' said Kitty Hennessy.

'And poor Áine never taken out a Mother's Day or Little
Women's Christmas in all her life!'

The pair of them clutching at each other over the great
wrong done to her. To his Áine! A bit rich coming from Bea
Doyle, who still started her car in second gear and took off with
the back bumper hopping off the road.

He had worked hard all his life, he wanted to tell them.
Áine was the one who thought eating out was a pure waste.
But let the auld biddies to their gossip. Let them think he was
sleeping on a mattress full of money.

'John, how are you?' The waitress appeared at his elbow.

Making a point of his name. He looked at her. She was one
of the Flynns. Or the Taggarts, as was. The mother would have
been in school with Ellen. Every one of that family worked in
the hotel at one time or another. They must have a conveyor belt
of them out in the store room.

'Still above ground,' he said, to soften her cough for her,
but she continued to hover.

'Will I carry the tray to the table for you?' she asked.

'I can manage, girleen.' Let her frown all she liked. His father, God rest his soul, called them all 'girleen'.

She followed him to the table with her two hands held out either side as though to speed him along. To be young was to be in a hurry. Ellen was the same. Always pressing the door release on the microwave straightaway instead of letting it sit the advisable minute.

The young one's concern wrong-footed him. Or his table was slippery. Or the tray was wet. Or some damn thing. The glass slid, icy water sloshing onto chair and carpet. He watched the girl swipe and blot. It wouldn't kill her to heft a bit quicker, time was ticking on and Ellen would be phoning shortly.

'You'll let me carry it for you next time, John,' she said.

The cheeky pup. He skipped the coffee altogether. Let them think he was sour over it. Let them wonder if they'd lost his business.

The hill up to the graveyard was slow going but pleasant enough, with the seagulls perched on the rigging of the boats and shouting out everything they could see. Áine loved that sound, she told him, when they were walking home from a dance early in their courting.

'The lonesomeness of it makes me feel dramatic,' she said, linking his arm. The vodka and orange was showing on her. 'Bury me where I can hear seagulls.'

'I will,' he said, where another man might have thought her forward to be imagining her future with him in it.

The graveyard gate opened silently. He closed it. Opened it again. The creak was gone. Patch Mullan that kept the place must have appreciated the word in his ear yesterday. Things had to be minded or they fell apart. Nothing surer. He took the path two-thirds of the way in, then cut between the headstones, careful where he walked. The grass was inching upwards, not quite over the lip of the stone kerbing. Not quite untidy. No need to say it to Patch yet, only just keep an eye on it. The last cut of the season had a very small window, it would catch out most people.

He spent a few minutes with Áine. 'Come up to me when you feel like it,' she had said. 'No pilgrimages.' Still steering him even though she was drifting in and out by then. *One in two,* the consultant said the day of the diagnosis, pausing as if to give him the chance to volunteer in her place. As if he wouldn't have given everything he had.

He picked up the stray pebbles and put them back on Ted and Alice Twomey's grave where they belonged, then spat on his hanky to get the worst of the birdshit off the headstone. It would tickle Áine to know the seagulls liked her too. The streaks wouldn't lift all the way off, he'd have to bring some vinegar in a bottle to do it right. All the years of half-reading the paper while Áine watched her gardening shows on TV had taught him a few tricks. That would tickle her too.

'Afternoon, John.'

'Fine day for it, Connie.'

'Mild enough yet.'

'We can't complain.'

Duty done, they saluted and moved on. If he met the same six people every day, he would have the same conversation six times. Áine used to tease him that one day, for fun, he should start in on American foreign policy. The neighbours wouldn't know where to put themselves, she said. Only she made him promise he'd do it when she was there so she wouldn't miss being in on the joke.

He brought his watch up nearer his face to read the numbers. Coming up on one thirty. Ellen would phone in the afternoon, she had said, but that could be anywhere from two o'clock to seven o'clock. She never had an iota of time sense and often left him waiting a good hour for her to come out of teenage discos long years ago.

'I heard the national anthem forty-five minutes ago,' he would say as she hopped into the front seat, her coat in her hand and her eyes shining.

'Sure things were only getting started then,' she'd say, kissing his cheek. 'Will we stop for chips?'

And stop they would, no matter that the distance to his morning alarm was shortening by the minute.

He walked at a smart clip up home, arriving back in the kitchen at bang on one forty-five. He put the kettle on to boil for his coffee. Buttered two digestives and ate them. Turned the radio up so he could hear it. Turned it down again so as not to miss the phone when it rang.

Feargal Sharkey was singing about how good hearts were hard to find. Ellen had it for the first dance at her wedding, and when it came time for him to take over from Matt, she held out her hand for him to twirl her around the floor. Over her shoulder he could see the queue at the bar. Lord but some of those boys must have had a terrible thirst on them to be on their third or fourth or fifth already. And all of it coming out of his pocket. Mercifully, he had kept that thought to himself, turning her towards her mother and Matt and telling her instead about their own wedding day.

'Your mother walked up the aisle and she was the most beautiful girl I ever saw,' he said. 'Until today.'

It was true in spirit, if not in fact—he had come of age in the days of Brigitte Bardot and Sophia Loren—and it made Ellen happy, so what harm.

He hadn't seen her as radiant since.

He took out the brush and gathered the biscuit crumbs into a tidy heap in the corner, where the dustpan made short work of them. A man on his own had to keep the place right. He didn't want Áine arriving back to collect his soul for heaven, only to be distracted by inches of dust on the mantelpiece. She would insist on cleaning everything, wasting precious minutes in the hereafter. Were the minutes still precious if they were infinite? He could be finding out.

The bolt on the back door was stiffening with the oncoming cold and he gave it a drizzle of oil to keep it sweet. As he worked the cloth over the metal, the three o'clock flight to London passed overhead. On fine evenings, himself and Ellen used to take a flask of tea and drive half an hour to the viewing point at the crossroads behind the airport. There they would sit on the bonnet of the car, the setting sun warming their legs, the two of them snug and quiet inside the roaring.

At half past four, the evening news shows came on. *Drivetime.* The idea, he supposed, was that people caught up on everything important they might have missed during their busy day. Time in the car or the bus or the train repurposed into another form of activity. It was no wonder Ellen's conversation was always so taken up with telling him how tired she was. He took a tomato out of the fridge so the cold of it wouldn't hurt his teeth later and listened to an item about the refugee crisis. Poor misfortunates. Fleeing countries in their droves, leaving land and home in the hands of lunatics. It was a hard road for them and no mistake. Many more of them over here and the place would be unrecognisable, they said, but sure maybe that wouldn't be the worst thing.

The next item was the rising crime rate and he turned it off. Some days he wondered how despair hadn't young people lined up like lemmings on the Cliffs of Moher. *The Cliffs of Mohair*, Ellen used to call them, making a fall seem soft and inviting.

The day she told them she was moving halfway around the world, he listened in silence as Áine asked all the right questions. 'You're fierce quiet,' Ellen said then. 'Have you nothing to say?' He wanted to ask how long she had been planning this. He wanted to ask if all those times he was watching the planes landing, she was only looking at the ones taking off. Instead, he gathered wits enough to tell her it was a fine idea — the finest — and was rewarded with a hug.

After finishing his supper, he dried the plate, put it back into the press, then lifted the phone to listen to the dial tone for a split second. All in order. When Ellen phoned, he might ask her when the clocks went back. He'd have to make it clear he was asking about over there, that he knew the score here at home. He didn't want to seem loose or, God forbid, needy. Áine laughed at him that last time she came out of hospital, telling him he had stored up all his chat while she was gone. 'I needn't ask did you miss me,' she said. 'You're bursting like a double quilt stuffed into a single quilt cover.'

He could remind Ellen about the planes though. Tell her he remembered it fondly.

The night drew in and the heating came on, the house ticking and warming around him. On the television, people around the world were shooting and insulting and ignoring one another. When Ellen and the boy, Luke, came and stayed those final days, when Áine was making hard work of leaving them, she turned off the television every time the news came on. 'He's too small to see all that,' she said, forgetting she herself was reared on three bulletins a day. Did the boy know there was a world out there at all? Did he know what was happening in the stuffy heat of the back bedroom? But what could he do only let her have her way.

She was the same after the funeral, helping him to pack up Áine's things and fretting about how long it would all take. Whether she'd get it all done before her flight early the next morning. She found the Stanley hammer on the windowsill and gave out to him for leaving it lying around. He was going to tell her he was trying to hang fairy lights around the door so Áine would have something cheerful to look at, but her shoulders were high and cross with the effort of deciding things. He put it under the bed upstairs instead of back in the toolbox and it made him feel better to know if any little job arose in the house, he had the means to deal with it.

In bed, his feet were cold under the sheets. He reached for Áine's favourite blanket, which had survived Ellen's cull and still lay across the back of the chair on Áine's side of the bed. She never minded sharing. Used to be forever asking if he wanted a bite of this or that. Forty-six years of holding out her fork to him as though they were still courting.

His feet warmed slowly under the extra layer and by the time the radio told him it was tomorrow, he was fairly at ease, all things considered. Past midnight and Áine's birthday over for another year. Ellen must have mistaken the date. She would phone tomorrow, full of apologies.

'No harm done,' he would say, so that she might phone again without fear of feeling bad in herself.

Outside the window, a cat yowled and the moon hung steadfast. On his side, he could reach down and touch the hammer under the bed. The hickory handle that always sat so snug in his father's palm, and in his own, and in Luke's someday maybe, please God. He closed his eyes and waited for sleep.

*Kevin Barry*

# ON BUXTON HILL

L isten?
    The winter is making shapes down on that river. Trying
to carve itself from the air of the place. And it's colder again
now in the house on Buxton Hill.

I fell into a heavy sleep in the afternoon and I'm trying to
come out of it still. I'm a bit sort of drooly and discombobulated.
People are at their walks now, that kind of hour, with their
dogs, and all the rest of it, and their voices come up to me from
the road, all very chatty and all very taken with themselves,
but not in a way that's a bother to me, or not unreasonably so.

My high windows? I'm very pleased about them still. Laid
out now, before them, like a lord, the old body thrown down in
front of me — the way sometimes you'd examine yourself as if
you were another. The long spindle legs, the pigeon chest, the
gentleman's parts that are still a source of foolish pride to me,
the odd morning.

I went over the wall on Tuesday night and robbed a bag of coal and I nearly caused permanent damage to myself hefting it back again — I think it was the mischief of the escapade heated me as much as the coal lying in dull embers now in the grate of the ornate old fireplace that's much too grand, really, for this house, in its present incarnation, all in flats, a waft of rent allowance off the place that would stall a horse and there are dotty people everywhere on this hill.

The boy above me?

Well, hardly a boy, he's fifties, lank blonde hair with a vaguely New Romantic-type fringe that I find unnervingly flicky, and a birdy little face on him, all beaked and full of surprise, and the accent is very ripe, very English, very fine — Oh good morning, good morning, I think I'll nip down the hill actually for a croissant, some coffee. Good man yourself. Nip away. Not the greatest pair of lungs on him, I'd say. Fairly wheezy when he arrives back up with the oily little bag of croissants. And the way that he says the word, with French intonation, dropping the 't' — sometimes it makes me smile and other times it makes me want to puck the cunt through the wall.

But he pads about very gently, I'd have to say, at all angles of the clock, on his unknowable business. The look of a gent who might take a drink in the evenings. Says Padre Pio. But the refuse sacks, certainly, would be *clinkety-clinking* and he off to the bins. He talks on the phone, in the hall, Wednesdays and Sundays, eight o'clock, very loudly and very pronounced, as though talking to an old dear, a mother some place, I suppose, in England. There is no apparent logic to the way people wind up on Buxton Hill. It is something that I've thought about and tried to puzzle out.

I went to a nightclub (of all places) on Tuesday, on Oliver
Plunkett Street, and I tried to chat up some women there.
Disaster. Well, not a disaster, I mean I wasn't arrested, or
laughed out of the place, and there were some encouraging
glances, I half-believed, for a while, not pity, really, and there
was one girl — woman — I told her she had lovely hands, and
she said that was an excellent try. She did have very elegant
hands — I might have stared at them a beat too long — and the
way she said *excellent* left me short of breath and I pictured
her playing a piano, in the mornings, in a flowing blouson, and
me strolling across the floorboards to her, barefoot, with a pot
of herbal tea. Sunlight on the boards. A chocolate-coloured
labrador? All that kind of thing. There was something of the
nurse about her, too, very clean, and kind, I'd say, though not
to the extent she was going to parade back up Sunday's Well
Road with me. A nurse would be ideal in a myriad of ways.
Ear, nose and throat. I'll put on an egg, I suppose. Night.

The father? He's super, he's flying around the place on the
bike again, there've been no more incidents, since. He seems
to be keeping all of that very well tamped down, since.

An egg, or even two — we'll go mad.

Ructions across the hall, of course. Your woman is giving
out to the small fella again. Now the small fella doesn't be
right. In my opinion. The eyes on the child are a bit... off, in
my opinion. As if they belonged to someone else at one time.
It's nothing to do with me. I only mind really when Freckles
comes into the picture. Freckles is the dog and apparently
pisses or shits the place in the middle of the night. FRECKLES!
She do be roaring. FRECKLES! And me lying there, across the
hall, trying to think about my poems. Or a play, apparently,
is what I'm supposed to be writing now. They'll all be waiting

on that. I think she gave me a look one night when I met her out
by the meters. I think she'd been out, she was kind of done-up,
which wouldn't be the norm. Says Omar Sharif. But there was
a look, I'm sure of it—this kind of... *how-ya?* Of course the
girl was probably half-trolleyed. Or on tablets. And wouldn't
it make a lovely family picture? Herself, myself, the small fella,
and Freckles. Wouldn't that make a fine Christmas? State
pathologist has been summoned. I'm nearly as well off out of
all that.

Talking of eyes?

I've decided against the eye patch. Frankly, it felt like I was
over-egging the look. With the eye patch. I'm not saying that I
won't, on special occasions, give the patch an old airing. Though
what those occasions might be I have no earthly idea. But as
an ongoing proposition? No. I mean that eye is lifeless since I
was a child and to be only lately covering it up? At twenty-nine
years of age? I mean it's not like it's ugly or unpleasantly guzzy
to look at. It's just a bit pale and sometimes a bit... watery-
looking. As if I have a leak out of the brain. But there's worse
off, I suppose, and doesn't our friend, Thom What's-His-Face,
out of Radiohead, have the same eye fucked on him, the left, so
there's hope for us all—Thom must be making any amount of
money. Perhaps we see the world differently, myself and Thom
out of Radiohead, with a useful skew. I'm not unhappy. I felt the
eye patch was too much, it was too... Mister Mysterious, you
know? I'm not unhappy, says he, and the tears streaming down
my face on Grand Parade yesterday evening.

What it was, I was after a showing, at the Capitol, of *Romeo
and Juliet* in the new DiCaprio version and I found it very
affecting and to an extent that was possibly a bit extreme. So I
said the best thing was what few pounds I had, I'd spend them

on myself and I'd try to make myself feel better. Out with me, the Western Road, into Reidy's Wine Vaults, the baked salmon put up in front of me, like a prince, and a glass of cold white wine. Nice few pints of Beamish after it. I might have cried a small bit again on the way home, by the Mercy.

In and out of it then all day today. Is it like it comes in waves, Dr Sheila McCarthy asked me. I said that seems to me like quite a prosaic way to describe it. But we're not great with each other generally, as of late. The last time I was in, Dr Sheila McCarthy took one look at me and said 'ambulance'. I turned on my heel and walked out the door, I wouldn't be listening to that at all.

I've had no more word from the landlord, so whatever's going on with that situation, you're barking up the wrong tree. He's odd with me yet since the summer. All I did was open up a view for the place. An aspect, I gave the place. Out of plain old-fashioned neighbourliness I took down those fucking hedges. Those hedges were a protection, he says, all flustering, those hedges were a windbreak against what's coming up from that river. They were full of rats, I says. And evil feeling, while we're at it, I didn't say, not willing to forfeit for no good reason an explanation of the way dark humours can settle into even our domestic vegetation. I'm not saying I shouldn't have told the man before I rented the chainsaw. But I was only clearing a view for the place, and I mean look at us now, it's as if the heavens are opening out before us all the way to the cricket grounds, across the park, and the rooftops, and the old Mental — oh, it's gorgeous, really, from up here, and never finer than on the winter mornings we'll be going into very shortly now, clear, bright and brisk, breathe it into yourself, from the armchair, panned out, a cup of tea, a small fire in the grate, the weakling sun in your face, the high windows. Royal, then.

Or at least the odd morning.

I don't need a lot to be able to continue as I am just now. The idea is to fall back into the scenery of things. Five minutes, on the button, I find is ideal for the egg, five minutes and it retains an unctuous character. If it's unctuousness you're after. Brown bread, cut from the loaf, scald the teapot and yes, womanly, I know, the sense of it, and the movement around these tidy rooms, but necessarily so, in men who live alone, who live without women. Despite their very best efforts in the nightspots of Oliver Plunkett Street. Necessary compensation in gesture and tone. Kind of thing. Night.

There's giving out, again, over — our woman, and the small fella. She'd have had him young, I'd say, she's only about twenty-five, maybe? Hard to be landed then with an odd little fella. He doesn't do much, after school, there are no friends that call, he do be just kind of gommin' around the place, he do be in the hall outside, sitting on the stair, strange little face on, and there are shades, I'm sure of it, that pass up and down that stair. And from not that long ago, I'd say maybe early sixties? But no interest in Freckles, really, the small fella, or in dogs generally, I tried to show him pictures of dogs. Eight years of age, I think, and already gone off into himself.

Our other friend, above, now, gently shuffling, again, aiming for the sideboard, clinkety-clink, very ripe, very well-schooled, the accent, but lovely — we'd always have a word out by the meters. About nothing. Night.

The comical thing about it all is it took me so long to realise that what I was doing, in effect, was building a nest up here. I found that I was increasingly drawn to skins and furs. I was seeing them everywhere. I bought a very fine, a very heavy sheepskin rug, undyed, from a butcher on North Main Street.

He'd obviously have an 'in' with sheep people. Have a farm himself, for all I know. They would do, often, butchers. He could have a place outside Buttevant or something. Up in the hills. Lovely. Lambs. All the rest of it. Soft rain in your face. Enya on the headphones. Search me. But the rug was fabulous, it took me an age to cut it up, and actually it smelt of rain, a kind of mineral tang. An age! On the floor. With the kitchen knife. I arranged and glued the bits then almost as this kind of frame around the high windows. And I mean the furs, furs are not so hard to track down as you'd imagine in Cork city — the charity shops! I've fox fur, badger, mink even, some kind of stoaty little fella, and all very nicely trimmed and dressed and arranged now around the windows. It was just an idle thought I had one day but I'm delighted with the way it's worked out. And the sense of it now is genuinely one of nesting, up here, on Buxton Hill, as though in a sweet eyrie, above the river, and above its valley.

The landlord not gone on it, of course. Are you making an ossuary, he says to me. I'm making myself comfortable, I says. I'm blocking draughts, those windows are shot, a man could turn around in this place and get a cold in his kidneys. If you want to talk about repairing or replacing those windows, then we can look again at the situation with the skins and furs. That put manners on him. The ossuary. There's one now for the play. *The Ossuary*, by... A marvellous innovation, advances the entire form. Sensation of three continents.

Oh?

Front door in.

Bootsteps in the hall.

A sense of angry gonads.

Didn't I know well enough to keep the lights out and leave the fire die down? Somehow. Don't move, don't breathe, boy — that have all the sounds of Toberty. Very authoritative.

I thought he was gone for good. October the 2nd since Toberty's been seen on the premises. I have four bails of bri-quettes gone from his back kitchen. The evidence is long de-stroyed but he'll have his suspicions and he has a brother in Cork jail for murder. I'm not saying that kind of thing runs in families. I mean runs-in-families is not an area any of us, around this place, want to get involved in. I could go to my father's house. But there's more dicey. Don't breathe — keep it dark.

Night.

I'm not saying Toberty is the devil but I would understand him to be on terms with the devil. On a kind of consultancy basis. I'm not saying for one minute I didn't deserve the beating, there is a thing even in a house such as this as privacy but am I supposed to lie there, all the length of the tormented nights, and ignore the maniacal screeching? Four in the morning and women being dragged through the hallway by the hair of their heads and some of these it has to be said are women who have shown up more than once. For the love of Toberty. At least so far as I could make out from the crawl space. Discovery of which led to the head being thumped off me. By Toberty.

Anyway.

We're into the night of it all again. And to be quite honest with you? I don't know if this place has the winter in it for me. Thickening, lately, I believe, the air of rancour and dispute, in this house, on Buxton Hill, at all hours, as the light thickens, as our friend said, as crow maketh wing toward the rooky wood, with Toberty screeching at his women, and Freckles gone apeshit, and your woman roaring, and the small fella gommin' away on the stairs, and shades passing this way and hither, and Clinky shuffling around with his flicky fringe and the birdy little head and the landlord in and out with a big blood pressure face on him, and me, lying there, all a-tremble, thinking, over and again, just the one plain thought, the one thought repeating —

*This is no kind of peace for a young man.*

What I would like very much is a small house of my own. Ideally it would have an aspect such as this one. I realise that I could hardly hope for these windows again. But a place where I could close the door on the world and deadbolt it and go each evening into a place silent as a lung, that I might sit among my own thoughts in a place of no distraction, and I want it to be above the city so that I can see the palm of the city fill up with its lights, because after all the winter will soon come, and the days as often will be grey and dark, and it's inhospitable, here, sometimes, unless we make our pods in which we can travel above it and ride through the skies of the winter until the year again turns on its slow wheel and brings us back to the springtime, again, and then, once more, the city will be made of birds and light.

*Oonagh Montague*

# DOG COLLAR

'I'm going out,' she says.

His brown eyes do not waver from her face. Twin pools of not a whole lot.

'If I leave you inside, you'll piss on every chair.' Amy does a quick scan of the kitchen and its silt of breakfast; butter-skimmed knives, half-empty cereal bowls, the smallest of milk-pools exclamation-marking the floor. A schoolbook lies sideways under a chair, weighted by a lone shoe.

The dog wags his tail. There's a cornflake stuck in it. The fridge is humming. On it is pinned her younger son's drawing of a crooked train, the passengers resolutely cheerful even as they tilt. One of the passengers is her. Amy knows this because he told her so last night while she bathed him. 'It's you, Mummy,' he said, 'with blue hair.' She had kissed his hands and quelled the urge to suck the blue stains from his fingers.

Amy looks outside. The garden is untidy with footballs and bubble wands, the hydrangea is beginning to flower. She looks back at the dog.

'If I leave you in the garden, you'll howl the neighbours round.'

He starts to tremble. The cornflake falls to the floor. The thought of picking it up exhausts her.

'You're a shit dog altogether,' she says, but cheerfully, so as not to upset him.

Sid looks like a happy dog. He's a small terrier with tufted black fur and a jaunty, uncut tail. There's a red scarf around his neck. The scarf and tail lend him a rakish come-at-me-life countenance, but this is not who Sid is. He's a furred barometer of grief, and wherever she goes, he is watching. When her mood dips, he begins to tremble, trailing her from room to room, studying her face as if she were the weather and he a lone skiff. On the days when tears she doesn't feel pool at the corners of her eyes, Sid finds a shoe of hers and pees in it. If, like today, she has waited till the house empties, till her husband has left for work and the boys for school, waited till the door clicked shut, the air stilled and she with it, so that she can let her smile slide off her skin into the breakfast things, Sid begins to whimper, and the sound of it fills her with a quiet and pointless rage.

Right now, Amy has something she needs to do. She reaches for her coat, hooked on the back of the kitchen door.

'Okay, Sid. I'll bring you with me.'

He brightens immediately, powering down the hall as she gathers her keys and the lead from the hall table. She takes a fast, furtive look in a small mirror beside the framed photo from three summers ago, her face lining momentarily up alongside theirs, her eyes blue to their three pairs of brown, laughing with their feet in the sea. She loves this photo, how all three looked up just as she called out to them. *Click.*

Amy lets the dog out, pushing one arm and then the other into her sleeves, watching Sid race in tight circles around the gravel as she closes the door. She avoids clocking the dual gouges in the stones, signs of her husband's mood that morning, still furious about the dent in his Mercedes. His gold Mercedes.

Last night, she really hadn't been able to see a mark after the kid had rolled into her at the traffic lights. When her head had shunted forward sharply, just missing the wheel, she had felt instantly guilty, wondering what she had done wrong. From behind her, a young lad in a Nike t-shirt and vulnerably tight jeans had stepped out of the Toyota now nestled softly into the back of her husband's car. She got out to meet him.

'I forgot the handbrake,' the boy was saying, his words coming fast, hands lifting and falling like birds. 'It's my first car. I barely touched you. I just bought it. I'm driving it home.' She had seen her sons in the tremulous stance of him. She instantly forgave him, even though he hadn't said sorry.

'It's okay,' she said. She looked at the car. 'There's no mark.' There wasn't, that she could see. 'It was an accident. Go on away home.' She felt fine. It was fine.

'Come, Sid,' she calls, holding the lead up. He ignores her, finding instead a tiny hassock of primroses to piss on. She feels resentment on their behalf.

'Come on, Sid,' she says again, her voice low, soft. Still he ignores her.

She speaks louder. '*Sid. Come here.*'

This time he skulks towards Amy, belly low to the ground, head down as if to ward off a blow. She has never hit Sid. Not once. Yet this is a thing he has always done. When he does it, as he does several times a day, grovelling and whimpering, Amy is secretly plagued by the creeping urge to punt him clear over a wall. Instead, she clips on his lead and they begin the walk to St Anne's. Above them the sky is a bright, glaring grey and she regrets not taking her sunglasses. Sid, now, is delighted, oddly happiest when leashed to her side. He snuffles enthusiastically at corners and Amy tugs him gently along, thinking about Father David.

Seven years before, when she had applied to marry in her local church, it had brought her into Father David's unusual orbit. From their first conversation on the steps of St Anne's, a small church with a famous set of bells, she felt at ease in the man's presence in a way that surprised her. He was so much more than she expected of a cleric. Maybe, she thinks, guiding Sid around a collection of bins, it was because he wasn't just a cleric, he was also a father and a husband. She doesn't believe in God, and Father David has never asked her to. He had accepted her, just as she was.

He must be one of the cleverest and kindest people she has ever met. His sermons leave her feeling smarter than when she arrived. He is a man in constant forward motion — striding, pacing, throwing his leg over his bicycle — except for when he is listening. That was what she noticed that first day. When he listened to her, he was the stillest thing; domed head tilted slightly, wide grey eyes on hers. When, months and several meetings later, Father David had raised his hand on her wedding day to bless the congregation, Amy had felt actually blessed. She had wondered if the others around her felt a similar peace, including her father, sitting close by. That morning, when her father had arrived to give her away, she had had to beg him to climb into the wedding car. He had stood on the steps of the family home he had left years before, complaining that she was barring him access.

'I just want a quick look. For old time's sake.'

'Come on, Dad, please.'

'He can stay outside. He just wants to see what he can pilfer,' her mother had said from inside, leaving her, a white-frocked, flower-carrying bouncer, alone on the street with him.

Amy waits to cross at the lights, keeping Sid close in case he steps into the road. She remembers clearly the damp May morning after her first son was born, when she had been pleased and surprised to find Father David on her doorstep, in his cleric's collar and coat.

'Too wet to cycle,' he had announced, as he came in for the first of many visits, of long conversations held over the top of her first, and then her second baby's sleeping head. These chats had punctured the exhaustion of motherhood, returning Amy to the world as together they discussed life, politics, childhoods and bicycles. She had, from that very first meeting on the steps, continued to speak frankly to this man, in front of whom she felt safe enough to be vulnerable. As her boys grew and she returned to her work as a freelance journalist, Father David still appeared at her door every few months. Until a few days ago, when he had phoned to say he was leaving the parish.

'Will you come see me in my office before I go?'

Amy had been cooking dinner and simultaneously trying to write a piece on parenting while the boys whined in stereo. She had closed her eyes, shutting out the laptop, the children and the kitchen to focus on his voice.

'You're leaving?'

'Yes. There's something I want to ask you.'

Amy walks up Shandon Street, threading through the small lane at the bottom of St Anne's. Together, she and Sid take the eleven steps to the doors, turning left into the walled garden of the church. She ties him to the lichen-spackled gravestone of a dead parishioner.

'I can't take you inside, Sid. You'll christen his office.'

This is a thing Sid does at other people's houses. He will be safe here. Tucked in off the street. There's a slight breeze. The sound of bells drifts down. Sid is trembling hard, eyes fixed on hers. He whimpers, and Amy feels an answering flare of irritation.

Father David's office door is to the left of the main entrance. She knocks softly, feeling younger than her forty-one years.

'Come in,' he says.

She opens the door to see him at his enormous desk in a tiny room, covered with piles of documents and books. His desk looks like what she imagines his brain to be; busy, full.

'Ah, hello.' He looks up at her, his face familiar and dear. 'Here, take a seat.' He lifts his backside from his swivel chair and begins moving things off the only other seat in the room. An upright wooden one to the left of his desk, directly facing the window. He indicates she sit.

'Hello Father David, how are you?'

'I'm... well, I'm this...' He waves a vague hand at his desk as he lowers himself back down.

As she settles herself, he turns back to his desk and begins to scan the sheet in front of him. On the desk is his gold fountain pen. This pen and his bicycle are two things that go everywhere with Father David. Both are old and loved. She wonders what it is like to have things like that, that you love and don't lose. She can't hold on to anything. She once left a beautiful ring from her grandmother on the number eight bus, walking away from it laid out on the seat beside her watch and bus pass. She often does things like that, able later, uselessly, to recall her hands moving unbeknownst to herself, performing rituals she isn't privy to. That she still has her wedding ring is an anomaly. She brings her mind back and focuses on him. He isn't looking at her, but still at the page, scanning down till he reaches the end. He picks up the gold fountain pen, takes off the top and makes a definitive tick, putting the lid back on and laying it down beside the sheet of paper, lining both up neatly. An interesting choice, she thinks, given the state of the rest of the room.

Aware of being silent as she watches him, she goes to fill the space. 'Moving house and business, it's a lot. You need me to help?'

'No,' he says, so emphatically she feels put out.

She studies the side of his face, uptilted nose and greying sides over his white cleric's collar. She begins to wonder why she is here, backstage. This is nothing like their usual informal chats over tea in her living room. Father David turns to look at her, using the swivel of his chair to bring himself fully around to face her, his hands on either arm rest, palms facing upwards.

'It's all in hand,' he says, 'I do need something from you, though.'

She leans back into her chair, waiting for him to expand. Above them come the unsteady chimes of what may be 'Three Blind Mice', punctuated with long pauses and clanged wrong notes. St Anne's bells can be rung by anyone, making the church a tourist spot. She played the bells last summer with her boys. It was fun. Now, she wonders how he ignores it. Maybe that's why he's leaving.

'Right,' he says. 'I'm going to ask you a question.'

Bong, Bing, say the bells.

He is looking right at her. Amy wills herself to look able for this level of seriousness, pushing down the urge to crack a joke.

'I want you to not answer straight away,' he says.

She feels the itch to laugh. Tamps it down.

Bing, bong, say the bells.

'You're going to sit and think about the question for exactly twenty minutes,' he says. 'At the end of that time, you'll give me your answer. How does that sound?'

*It sounds terrible.*

'Sounds okay,' she says.

Bong, BING, say the bells.

'You ready?'

*She isn't ready.*

'I'm ready.'

'Are you happy?' he says.

Amy opens her mouth to respond immediately — this is easy — but Father David lifts his hand. He consults his watch, patting the face with his index finger to indicate that he has marked the time, then turns back to face his desk. He picks up another stack of pages and begins to sift through them.

Bong, Bing, BONG, say the bells.

She stares at his back.

BING.

*What a stupid question. Of course she's happy.*

BONG. BONG.

*This is ridiculous. She is a grown woman sitting in a chair, looking at a man's back as if she's in detention.*

BONG.

*Of course I'm happy.* Amy thinks. *I have two children who are healthy. I have a job and a husband and all my own teeth.*

BING, Bong, Bing, Bong, say the bells.

*How long more?*

Amy filches out her phone and checks the time. It's been three minutes. *Christ. Another seventeen to go.* She has her answer already.

BONG. BING. BING. BING.

The bells are now attempting 'Frère Jacques'. She feels sorry for them. They must hate themselves. *How has he listened to this all day?* She studies his back, his elbow moving gently as he writes, the hair thinning at the back of his head, the trimmed bit at the nape.

Poor Father David.

BONG. BONG. BONG.

*Fucker. Why is he making her do this? She hasn't time to be sitting here thinking. She is a busy woman, a mother, a journalist, a wife. Busy. She is a happy, busy woman.*

At that moment, Amy becomes aware that there's another sound poking at her.

BONG. BONG. Bing. Yap.

Under the bells and just to the left of the scratching of Father David's pen, there it is again. She turns to the window. There's only a grey stone wall outside. The sky is an unhelpful colour.

BING. Yap.

She realises the sound has been a constant for at least— she checks the time again — six minutes. Her brain hands her the realisation that it's a dog. It's a dog barking. It's Sid.

BONG. BONG. Yap, yap.

*Suffering Divine Jesus this is going to be the longest twenty minutes of my life.*

BONG. Yap. BONG. Bing. Bing. Yap.

This is so embarrassing. Father David must be able to hear her stupid dog. Amy knows he's stupid because he's her dog and everything she does always ends up weird and hard to manage. But usually, she manages just fine. She does, it's just that she forgets sometimes and approaches things thinking they'll run smoothly, like borrowing his car. She shouldn't have done that. She should have known it would go badly.

YAP. BING. Howl.

*Oh no. He's branching out.*

She looks again at Father David's back. He's still writing. He doesn't appear to be hearing any of this. Maybe he's deaf? No, that's not it. Maybe it's that he's so zen he can block everything out. She tries to tune into the sound of his pen. That, at least, is a good sound, the sound of industry. She is going to miss him. He is her friend.

*Although good friends don't ask you questions and then not let you answer them.*

Yap. Yap. BING. BING. BONG. HOWL.

*This is actual hell.*

Yap. Howl. BONG. BONG. BONG.

*Why can't I just tell him my answer now? Of course I'm happy. Or I would be if the dog would just shut up. He's the problem. He's a terrible dog. He's why she can't even have nice shoes.*

*Oh.*

'This is why I can't have nice things.' That's what her husband had said the night before. 'You're why.'

She was standing in the doorway of the living room, still in her coat, telling him about the boy rear-ending his gold Mercedes. He had interrupted her to say it. Amy had stopped talking then; instead, she had watched as Sid slowly, carefully got up from his place by the sofa to tiptoe from the room, hugging the walls as he went. As her husband pushed past her to check his gold Mercedes for marks, she had noticed that she was trembling. She could see it in her fingers as she trailed behind, watched him circling furiously, finding nothing.

*Something had been snagging at her.*

When he had started shouting, still circling, Amy had held the front door almost shut, so the boys would not hear. She had felt a kind of relief then, because once the shouting started, she no longer had to worry about it starting. He would shout and she would cry. He would go to the spare room and stay there for the night. The next day he would not talk to her, unless she made him a cup of tea and gave him a kiss, tried to cajole him back to her. She would do that. She would apologise for everything.

But something was still snagging at her...

'You didn't ask if I was okay,' she said.

He was still shouting, so she said it a second time.

'You didn't ask me if I'm okay.'

He looked at her then. Amy had recognised that he was side-stepped, set off-kilter by her words. She had wondered as she watched his face how he would swivel, reframe, make it into something else, but he didn't. Instead, he went back into the house, going straight to the spare room, the one they had painted a beautiful shade of Nantucket blue together. He slammed the door.


'Well?'

She looks up.

Father David's tone is gentle. He is watching her, having turned full in his chair, his hands holding each other in his lap. In her lap her hands are moving of their own accord, like small birds. She looks down at her stippling fingers, the bitten nails, the fluttering paleness of them. She wills them still, feeling his gaze as she spans back over their shared conversations, side by side on her sofa. She wonders if maybe they have never been friends. Perhaps he has just been doing his job. Perhaps he has been looking out for her all this time. She thought they were friends, but maybe this is better.

'Amy?'

She looks up and right into his eyes.

She takes a breath.

*Eileen O'Donoghue*

# HIS SHOES

The Sergeant drives down the hospital hill from the barracks, around the back of O'Connor's pub and parks beside a row of empty kegs. Up at the station the lads call the place Accident & Emergency. It needs more than a lick of paint. The beer garden is haggard-looking, tired furniture, cigarette butts everywhere mixed into the gravel. Cap in his hand, he looks back at the squad before he steps inside.

In the dim light he makes out Timmy O'Connor with a tea towel over his shoulder, stacking glasses from a dishwasher tray, steam rising, chatting to two customers at the bar counter. Farrell, of course, a regular smart-arse, still drinking at lunchtime after it cost him his job in the boy's school across the road. The other man is a stranger, must be passing through. Timmy's wife, Anne, is putting fresh coasters under their pints.

Timmy straightens up, a pint glass upside down in his hand.

'Timmy,' the Sergeant nods at him. 'How's business?'

'What can I do for you, Sergeant?'

Timmy knows him long enough to call him Don, but he's keeping it formal. He puts the pint glass back in the tray, dries his hands on the tea towel and moves to where the Sergeant has stopped at the opposite end of the bar from Farrell and his drinking buddy.

'Just wanted a word.' He fingers the ribbon-band along the inside of his cap.

'Sergeant,' Farrell calls. 'I hear your young fella is off to Templemore.'

'Mind your business, Farrell,' he says. 'That your blue Skoda outside? Scratch on the left bumper, no tax on it?'

'Sure, I was only congratulating you.' Farrell smirks, raises his pint.

Anne turns her back to fill a whiskey for Farrell, then leaves through a door beside the till.

'Somewhere quiet, maybe?' The Sergeant turns his attention back to Timmy.

'Here is fine,' says Timmy, placing the tea towel on the counter between them.

He watches Farrell, keeps his voice low.

'Look, this business on Saturday night...'

Timmy cuts him off, speaking louder than the Sergeant would like, 'Would that be the business of your Cian holding my son down so Chris Ryan could break his jaw and knock out his teeth? That the business you're talking about, is it?'

'I'm here,' he says, arms out, a gesture of offer.

'You're here because your lad is off to Templemore. To make sure that happens.'

'I wanted your account of it.'

'Well, now you have it.'

'Maybe when you've had a few days to see how things are, we can talk then.'

'What? So you can offer me a few bob to fix his teeth? Turn a blind eye to the pub for a few weeks?'

'They're young lads, Timmy. Trying to make their way. He deserves a chance.'

Timmy gives the counter a wipe, then leans both hands against it, shoulders less defensive now. 'Look. Everyone knows ye had ye're dark days, Don. But you don't need me to tell you that boy is no guard.' Timmy meets his eye now. 'He's not Shane.'

In the car, the Sergeant indicates left to go back up the hill to the barracks, changes his mind, flicks the right indicator, turns down onto Percival Street. His heart is still thumping at the sound of it. Shane. Like the whip crack of a bullet passing your ear. When he died, the questions became a mantra. How's Ellen coping? Cian doing alright? Do ye need anything? But they never said his name. Then came the platitudes. Good days and bad days I suppose. Take it handy. Mind yourselves. Early days yet. Now, almost three years later, people nod at him in that dark way, acknowledging the mark on him before avoiding him altogether. He navigates through the Square, one hand on the steering wheel, one on the gear stick, giving a glance at the fruit and veg market outside Kelly's Bar, eyes peeled out of habit through the small stretch of Main Street. It's quiet everywhere, waiting for the slog of school children to spill out of the two primary schools at three o'clock, the older ones from the Tech and the Convent at four. Shane and Cian were once part of that caterpillar of blue and grey that huddled and moved as one being, downhill from the boy's school, dissecting and dispersing through the Square, taking different routes home. Over the bridge now, the river on his left, he takes a right onto Earl Street, up past Paddy O'Callaghan's garage, heading out the Freemount Road.

He parks the squad around the back of the house, lifts the handbrake and pulls himself out of the driver's seat. In the utility, the washing machine whirrs uphill into a spin as he comes in the back door. The rocking noise of it moves him on into the kitchen. He takes off his cap and rubs his hair into place, what's left of it. He hasn't had a bite since seven this morning. Not much mind for it now. Ellen won't be home from school for another half hour, longer if she stops at the SuperValu.

There's a mess on the table and the hall door is wide open.

'Cian?" He shouts at the gaping door.

*The Sun* is sprawled on the table next to a cereal bowl and coffee mug, a spoon radiating splashes of milk onto the wood. He pushes the newspaper out of his way and his son's phone appears. Christ's sake. He's probably gone back to bed and he's supposed to have the kitchen clean for his mother when she comes in. In his hand the screen flashes half a message from *Christy Ryanaldo — keep your mouth shut lad...* He doesn't know the code for the phone, drops it back on the table. Only two weeks to training and this happens.

In the hall, the newel post is cold under his hand.

'Cian! Get up,' he calls up the stairs.

'What?' The bedroom door is shut.

'Are you up?'

'I'm not working 'til four.'

'Can you open the door when I'm talking to you?'

The door opens a crack. 'Fuck's sake.'

'What?'

'Nothing, I'm coming.'

Bare feet, in orange flip-flops, cross the landing so he goes back to the kitchen. At the window over the sink, he lifts a framed photo off the sill, his own father and himself, both in uniform at his passing out ceremony all those years ago. His father's mortuary card is tucked into the bottom corner of the frame, taking a chunk out of their handshake. Ellen has a tea-light burning for his anniversary this week. They were close, his father and Ellen, always having a laugh at his expense, ganging up on him. He was too serious, too strict, had no give in him. He'd tell his father that was alright in his day. The other end of the sill is devoted to Shane. The permanently lit candle, the photos cut out in different sizes, stacked and standing against a wooden crucifix, the arms appearing to enfold all in front of it. Their shining boy. How many times has he pictured Shane in uniform, daydreamed about recreating the father-son handshake in the photo he holds in his hand. It comes to him as easily as picturing a cloud in the sky.

He puts the photo back on the sill, behind the flickering tribute.

'Thought you were on duty.' Cian is behind him.

'Were you out Saturday night?' The Sergeant turns.

'What?' Cian reaches for his phone on the table.

'Put the phone down. Were you out on Saturday night?'

'Yeah.'

'With who?'

'The lads.'

'Chris Ryan?'

'He was out.' Cian folds his arms across his chest.

'You were mentioned at the station this morning.'

'There was a bit of a scrap. Is that what you want to know?'

'Where?'

'Outside the chipper. Nothing serious.'

'You sure now?'

Cian stands there, in his *DOWN WITH THIS SORT OF THING* hoodie and his club shorts, green and white, the club Shane captained at under sixteen. And those orange flip-flops he can't stand. When did men start wearing flip-flops?

'A few of the minor team were pissed, acting stupid. One of them shaped up to Chris, so I shoved him back, for his own good. Check the cameras if you want.'

'Is that all?'

'Jesus! Okay. Chris sees the same lad, down by the old cinema, meeting some girl there. So he starts messing, makes a comment about having a go off the girl and your man loses it and goes for Chris. I held him off, told him to calm down. Chris gave him a few punches.'

'Just so we're clear, who's the boy?'

'One of the O'Connor's.'

'How old?'

'Dunno. Eighteen?'

'He's sixteen. Got his jaw wired yesterday.'

'No way he was that bad! He was getting up for more when we left him. The girl was hysterical, throwing stuff at us, her shoes and her bag and shit. Chris kept at it, mocking her, but I got him away, took him home. That's it.' Cian sits into a chair, legs stretched out in front of him. 'Shit. Look, I've told you everything.'

'Shit, is it? Is that what you have to say? After all I've done to get you in. Do you want to stay in your shit job in the hotel? Is that it?' He turns away, to calm himself.

'How many times did I tell you to stay away from Chris Ryan, that he was only a pup, out looking for trouble. You only had to keep the head down for another two weeks.'

'Did Luke give a statement?' Cian asks.

The Sergeant faces him, holds his gaze, 'Not yet.'

'He won't either. It's their word against ours. Two against two.'

Ellen's car disturbs them, wheels rolling to a stop behind the house. She's early. The back door opens and she's calling, looking for help with the shopping. They move at the same time, almost colliding, the boy's shoulder not quite reaching the Sergeant's.

She's struggling with two bags, pushing the back door in with her shoulder. He takes them from her. 'You're early, love.'

'I wasn't feeling great. The SNA said she'd supervise the last half hour.'

She changes her shoes inside the back door. 'Why is the washing machine on?'

'Some eejit spilled red wine on my hoodie Saturday night.' Cian, leaning in the doorframe, answers her.

'Is it on a cold cycle?' She puts her bag and keys on the worktop, puts a stray rib of hair behind her ear.

But Cian's gone out for the rest of the shopping and the Sergeant says, 'Why don't you put on the kettle and I'll give him a hand.'


The old kettle starts to hum, the noise escalating slowly. Cian puts his breakfast things in the dishwasher, jamming the dishes into the over-full machine while the Sergeant puts away the bread and cereals, leaving vegetables and a butcher's bag on the table, presuming that's dinner. Ellen places three mugs on the worktop and the bubbling water finishes with a click.

'Something's wrong,' she says, blotches of colour rising on her neck.

He tells her that Chris Ryan was in a fight on Saturday night, that Cian was there and he's just asking him about it.

'Are you hurt?' She goes to the boy, touches his cheek, looking for a mark.

'Stop.' Cian shrugs her off.

'Chris Ryan for God's sake. Why didn't you let him at it and walk away?'

She puts a tea bag in each mug, splashes in boiling water, takes a teaspoon from the drawer and stops. 'There's more, isn't there?'

The Sergeant takes the spoon out of her hand and squeezes the tea bag in each cup, dropping them individually into the bin under the sink. It's full to the top.

'A young lad got hurt,' he tells her. 'One of the O'Connor's, from the pub.'

'One of Anne and Timmy's? Is he alright?'

'His jaw is broken, lost a few teeth. But he'll be fine.'

She takes the cup he offers but puts it away from her, on the table. 'What happened. How did it start?'

Cian's on his phone, typing with his thumbs. 'Luke started it. He was pissed, celebrating after some match.'

'Isn't he underage? He shouldn't be drinking at all. It's so dangerous.'

'We don't know for a fact that he was drinking,' the Sergeant says. He wants to distract her from an escalating panic about the dangers lurking everywhere.

'Please, Don. Stop being the Guard for one minute, will you. Is Cian in trouble?'

'No. There's no official complaint, so a charge is unlikely.'

'A charge?' She raises her hand to her throat.

Cian interrupts them. 'If anyone is in trouble, it's Chris, not me.'

'Sure, what chance has he? The house he comes from.' She wraps her arms around herself.

Nobody speaks, and the sounds of the house grow louder, a clock ticking, the fridge humming, a broadcaster's low monotone from the radio. The washing machine hits its final spin, whining higher and faster until it reaches its top note, then stops with a thump of clothes landing in the drum.

Cian's phone is constantly buzzing.

'Did you eat?' she asks him.

'I'll get something at work.'

'Go and change then,' she says. 'Your father can wait and drop you down.'

'Whatever.' Cian crosses the room, the suck of his flip-flops slapping against the new silence.

Ellen closes the door after him.

'Was he in the fight?' she asks.

'He did enough.'

'Will it delay his training?'

'No,' he said, 'I'll sort it.'

She sighs, lets her hands fall to her sides.

'I called in there at lunchtime,' he tells her. 'To the pub.'

She doesn't answer.

'Timmy was awkward enough.'

'It's his child,' she says, but already he feels her drifting from the conversation.

'Do you ever think…' She trails off.

'Think what, love?'

'He could have been in college by now. He could have been out of the house. All this waiting around…'

He rinses his mug, lifts the bin bag out by the yellow strings, pushing down hard on the contents, takes all the air out of it and knots it tight. On the windowsill, the candle flickers under his father's photo. With his free hand, he lifts the mortuary card from the frame. The picture on the cover is his father's Garda cap resting proudly on the tricolour draped over his coffin. In the weak sunlight, he spots a smudge and wipes it clean with his thumb.

He picks up the rubbish to take it out. 'You alright, love?'

But she's gone now, even though she's standing two feet away from him.

He knows she's waiting for them to go, that she'll pick up the photos of Shane, one by one, as soon as he's gone out the door. She'll probably go up to the graveyard. It's a blessing and a curse how close it is to the house. A comfort to Ellen in the beginning when she went up there at daybreak to light the candle in the little lantern, him following her the mornings it poured, to take the wet lighter from her hands.

When he came to town, his uniform still hanging on his skinny frame, he hadn't expected it, to meet her, to marry so soon. Before he knew it, his wedding ring had worn a groove on his finger and they had two boys in primary school, fighting to wear the cap of his uniform every chance they got, to get a drive in the squad, put the siren going. Theirs was a small neighbourhood half a mile from town, a line of twelve houses, all built on sites bought from the farm behind, except for the two Garda houses at the end of the row, where he'd started out as a stranger. When it was time to settle, he'd chosen the neighbours he already had. They'd built extensions and watched All Irelands together, jump-started each other's cars, and knew too much about each other in general. Their children had travelled as a band of harmless trouble-makers, knocking down bales in Haulie Barry's field to make forts, fishing for minnows with their red-net poles on the stony banks of the Allow, fed together in whatever house they landed in at tea time. It would be someone else's house the following day.

That awful night, he'd appeared at the side of their bed, said his head was bad, something was wrong. After that fucking match. A stupid friendly that didn't even count for anything. It hadn't looked like a bad bang. And he'd played on. He was seventeen, fit as a flea, already tipping six foot. He'd be fine. Of course, he would. When the ambulance crew took him out the front door, unconscious and wrapped in that mottled, pink blanket, he'd still had hope. But the neighbours, who'd seen blue lights on the road and stood silently in their bedclothes in respect, understood it before he did. They were saying their goodbyes.

Cian comes back into the kitchen, changed for work, white shirt, black pants, green converse shoes peeping out. No jacket. Ellen used to remind him to wear one.

'Can you wear those at work?' the Sergeant asks.

'What?'

'Green shoes.'

Cian gives him a look, like are you serious, shakes his head, makes that sarcastic smile.

'They're his shoes, aren't they?' he says.

'Is that a problem?'

'No. Unless your mother…'

Ellen turns, suddenly focused. 'Were you in his room?'

'The shrine, you mean?' Cian says.

'Take them off.' She starts to shake. First her shoulders, then all the way down to her hands.

He moves in between them. 'It's alright, love.'

'They're his shoes.' She's crying now.

'His shoes. His room.' Cian is shouting now. He's at the windowsill, toppling the photos and the crucifix off the sill, into the sink. 'He's fucking dead! And this house is a fucking grave.'

'Shut up! Shut up!' Ellen is wailing now.

He puts his arms around his wife, moves her, looks back at Cian in warning. 'Not another word.'

She doesn't want to go upstairs, resists him weakly before giving in, her breathing still ragged.

'Lie down for a bit, love. I'll talk to him.'

Their room is dark, the bed unmade, the curtains still closed since this morning. She lies down on top of the bed covers.

'Sometimes I wish it was him. Not Shane,' she says.

He sits on the bed, the air in the room stale and stifling.

'You don't mean that.'

'Don't you ever think it?'

He feels her searching his face but he won't look at her. And he remembers the word *náire* from school. It means so much more than the English translation. Shame.

'I'll take him to work.'

She turns away from him, her breath coming in shaky gasps.

He puts his hand on her back. 'I'll come back as soon as I can.'

Cian is outside, leaning against the squad, smoking, still wearing the shoes. The Sergeant knows it's a challenge, that he's looking for another fight. He lets it go, takes the keys out of his pocket.

'I'll walk,' Cian says, dropping the cigarette on the ground, covers it with his foot.

'You've no jacket and it's going to pour.'

'It won't kill me.'

'Get in, please. We can talk.'

They sit into the car together, closing the doors just as drops gather and spread on the windscreen. Tired now, his eyes blur like the glass in front of him and he turns on the wipers. He doesn't know how to start the conversation. After a minute when neither of them speaks, he starts the car and pulls out of the driveway. He follows the curve of the road, past the new housing estate on the right, where they broke the old stone wall. The patch-up on either side of the wide entrance is a poor job, grey cement pale and wrong against the dark colour of the original wall. Behind the old Protestant church, the sky makes an attempt to brighten but in town the crows are huddled on solid branches, sheltering. On the bridge, he passes another squad, flashes his lights in salute. Back on the steep rise of Percival Street, he pulls up on the kerb outside the hotel.

Cian reaches to open the passenger door.

'Wait a second, will you?' he says.

Cian doesn't answer him, but does as he is asked.

'Do you want it? The job, the uniform?'

'You're asking me now?'

He doesn't have to look at the boy to know there's a sneer on his face.

'Yes. I'm asking.'

'What else am I am going to do? After hanging around here for a year?'

'I'll have to ask the O'Connors not to press charges. Be under obligation to them. Do you get that?'

'And what? I'm supposed to be grateful? When it's you getting what you want.'

Cian gets out, slams the door and runs around the front of the squad to get in out of the rain. The back of his white shirt darkens in seconds, almost through to his skin before he disappears through the door of the hotel. The Sergeant sits, watching the wipers moving over and back, until he has to move. He indicates, checks his rear-view, sees the gold badge of his cap move across the mirror as he drives out and continues up the hill.

He parks at the station, goes inside to tidy up some paperwork and check his messages before swapping the keys of the squad for his own. The phones are busy and he's spared any chat. Off duty now, he points his old Toyota down towards the Square. The rain has stopped and rivulets of water flow down the gullies on both sides of the road. On the footpath, something catches his eye. Green converse step lightly, heading downhill, heels lifting in turn off the path. Above them Cian, and Chris Ryan, are lighting up cigarettes and laughing as they walk right past the door of O'Connor's pub.

*William Wall*

# THE FACE

I went out without my face. I never do that. It was the start of a bad day. I was in a terrible rush of course because the alarm never went off. I hardly had time to wash myself. If I'm not there at half eight I'm dead. I don't start until nine. He took one look at me and turned his back. That's the way the fucker is. Type that up, he says. He gave me six letters. I had to type them up before the first patient came. Naturally the first patient came early. They know we book three to each appointment slot. That's so he doesn't have any slack times. He fairly goes through them. Three minutes sometimes. Fifty guineas. Most people pay in pounds anyway. One of the letters was telling a man that he had cancer. I hate those ones. But he rattles them off. Letter to Mr X, Dear Mr X, I regret to inform you that the tests have come back positive.... Except positive means negative. You're going to die. The prognosis is disastrous. The roof is going to fall down on your head. I typed out the letter. I wanted to change the words to make them softer. Dear Mr X, I have some bad news I'm afraid. But I got in trouble before. I made a mistake in the words and afterwards the man to whom it was addressed made a joke about it. I was never so embarrassed in my life, don't you dare alter as much as a comma. He even wagged his finger at me. I am older than him. By just two years I know. But still. I am not a schoolgirl. He is not the head teacher. He is a doctor and I am his secretary. He does not seem to understand this relationship. He is a small bumptious man with a bald head. He drinks sherry. He and his wife drink sherry every evening. Their house overlooks the harbour and they drink sherry watching the comings and goings of ships and the sunset. They do not get on. It is a Victorian house. I was to marry a young medical student when I was twenty and when I still had my looks but his family wouldn't have me. He was keen enough but in the end of the day there was money involved and my father, God rest him, had only the butcher shop. I later heard he married a horsey woman with land. I live in a flat in Sidney Place, which is convenient to his consultancy rooms. But it's not convenient to me. There is no garden at the back. All the floors above mine are vacant and more or less derelict like half the city. I get leaks. There is only one other tenant. He lives in the basement flat. His yard is alive with rats. I suspect they go in and out by the pipes. He is an old man and he never goes out there. I tell him, Get the Rentokil in. He gives me the finger. Still and all he tips his hat to me in the hall. He's a gentleman. Mr Troy, I said, you know how to treat a lady. Comes by nature and costs no money, he said. I hear him coughing all the way down there. He asked me if I could get an appointment in a hurry and I said I could yes. So I fitted in one extra at the ten fifteen slot and the fucker never even noticed. Old Mr Troy came in. I put him in the chair beside the Superser and he spent his time warming his hands at it and talking about the miracle of modern inventions and the weather. Nobody really wanted to talk to him. When he came out he treated me to a full run-down of the examination while we were standing in the hall with the door open. The rooms are in a Georgian terrace. How's your whatsits, his nibs says to me, very well doctor and how's yours, nice and regular I hope. When he left I marked him paid. But his letter went out just like the others. It was easy to get him an appointment, but not so easy to get him into hospital. I tried. Eventually the doctor came out and asked me what I was doing. I explained that Mr Troy was a neighbour. He said it wouldn't matter a damn whether he got in or not, and frankly it was a waste of resources. I cried and he said, Think about it, you put old Troy in there to die and he'll take up a bed that a young man could use. That was worse. I started thinking I was the secretary to death. But I got Mr Troy in eventually. Then I missed his coughing. The way he used to say howsyourfather, been to see the council, that's a right howsyourfather. And the way he used to sing when he was cooking. Once he said to me, Pity I didn't meet you in my heydey, Miss Welch, with your beauty and my brains. He is a charmer. Then they sent him home again. They didn't do anything. I saw the consultant's letter. Having been fully informed of his condition Mr Troy opted not to undergo treatment. You find all of human life in a doctor's waiting room. First thing today we had a plumber and his wife (prostate, benign), a solicitor (bowel cancer, follow-up visit, operation regarded as a success), a terminal seaman (lung with secondaries) and so on. The seaman had been a ship's engineer. The doctor was querying asbestos but no evidence had been found in histology. He was eager for the seaman to take a case. He had a special legal notebook where he wrote down the details of anything he thought might end up in court. He sometimes asked me to contact people for legal advice. He liked making court appearances as an expert witness. He would take out the pad which was always in the middle drawer of his desk and say, Do you want to make a claim? If the patient said no, he would say, Let's fill out a report anyway just in case. They usually ended up making one. But this morning after the first batch of patients he came in again and right in front of an elderly colonoscopy (suspected tumour), he told me to go home and put my face on. We had words and then I walked out. On the front steps I thought should I go home or not? I turned right instead of left. I walked down Sidney Place and turned down the hill into the town. Everything was different. It was a working day but there was some kind of parade. There was pop music.

I finished up in Fitzgerald's Park. It was a sunny day and I was lucky enough to get a seat where I could see the speeches. It was under a tree. I appreciated the shade. My hearing is not the best but I thought the speakers were quite good. They were funny. Lots of people laughed. I don't know what they were laughing at because I couldn't hear the jokes. Some of them were dressed up but it wasn't a play. It reminded me of the Panto. A very nice young man sat beside me. Are you ok, he said to me. I just walked out of my job, I said, I'm a doctor's secretary. Like walked out walked out? he said. I didn't know what he meant. I said, He was horrible to me, he told me in front of the patients to go home and do my face. How do you mean do your face? My make-up, I said, didn't you notice? I came out without my face this morning.

The young man grinned. I didn't like the cut of that grin.

What are you smirking at? I said.

Do you want to get your face done, he said. There's a guy here doing it. Are you up for it?

I was flustered. He was a nice young man and the speeches had me in the mood. I'm nobody's fool, I knew what he was talking about.

Why not? I said. I'm sixty-five years of age and I'm going to get my face done.

And that was how I got the clown face. It was grease-paint. My father was in amateur theatricals. He trod the boards in Panto and he was Hardress Cregan in Boucicault's *The Colleen Bawn* which ran for six weeks at the Opera House. It was a triumph. I went every Friday for six weeks until I knew it by heart. Oh if I could hope that I had established myself in a little corner of their hearts, there wouldn't be a happier girl alive than The Colleen Bawn. I told the man who did my make-up and he was very interested. I told him the whole story of *The Colleen Bawn* from beginning to end. He said I was a ticket. I told him that my father, who was a schoolteacher, used to call me his Colleen Bawn. He said that was sweet. I said, You're too sweet to be wholesome. He laughed. When I had my face on the nice young man took me around and introduced me to his friends, some of whom were in full costume, and then we had a picnic. They had wine and beer and cider but I declined resolutely. I am teetotal. I did try one of their cigarettes which was quite nice actually though I am not a smoker — working for a cancer specialist and general purpose egomaniac you would be afraid of your life to smoke. It's not tobacco Miss Welch, the young man said, it's totally safe. We had a nice singsong afterwards and I sang one of my father's old favourites, 'Scenes That Are Brightest'. Then I noticed that it was evening and I thought I should go home. The grease-paint boy offered to take my face off but I said no, I was quite happy, I felt somehow at home.

But you can't just walk home like that, they said.

But I did.

It was evening time and people were closing shops. Young people were hurrying home. Cars were turning their lights on and the street lights were beginning to brighten up the old place. For a long time I forgot about the catalogue of things that people die from. I walked through town like someone else. I was the clown who knew nothing. People didn't even look at me. Apart from one little girl and her mother. I stopped and looked in the window of The Moderne and I did not know myself.

I saw Mr Troy standing at his door looking the other way. I was right beside him before he saw me. He started. Then he laughed. He laughed so much he had to steady himself. And then he started to cough. I helped him down to his flat. There was mould on the wall.

Jesus girl, he said to me, are you trying to kill me.

He was laughing when he wasn't wheezing or coughing.

I stood my ground and pointed my middle finger at him. I said: There goes the only man I ever loved. When he's here near by me, I could give him the worst treatment a man could desire, and when he goes away he takes the heart and all of me off with him, and I feel like an unfurnished house. This is pretty feelings for a girl to have, and she in her regimentals.

He pointed a crooked finger at me. Boucicault, he said. *The Colleen Bawn*, am I right or am I wrong?

You're right, Mr Troy, fair dues.

He took a bottle of whiskey and two glasses from the draining board. He passed one to me. I didn't take it. My father was given to it. It destroyed him. Mr Troy was still wheezing. He poured some whiskey for himself and tipped his glass to me. Here's to *The Colleen Bawn*, he said. I seen your father in it, God rest him, and you're as good yourself.

It was the happiest moment of my life.

*Danielle McLaughlin*

# ALONG THE HERON-STUDDED RIVER

He gripped the ice-scraper in his gloved hands, pulled it back and forth across the windscreen. A mist of ice particles rose up, settled upon the car bonnet. It was dark yet, but the sun was beginning to rise, tingeing the white fields pink. All around him the land was hard and still, the ditch that separated their property from the farm next door brittle-grassed and silver. In the distance he could see the line of trees that flanked the river, their branches dusted with a light powdering of snow. A heron stood beside the small ornamental pond, stabbing the frozen surface with its beak. The previous Saturday, Cathy had driven to the city and had returned with half a dozen koi, some of them bronze and tea-coloured, others grey. He had watched her release them, dazed and startled, into the pond. Dropping the ice-scraper, he clapped his hands and the heron rose up and flew away.

The house was a dormer, facing south towards the river, set into a hollow in the field. From where he stood in the driveway, it looked like a Christmas ornament, frost clinging to the roof, condensation rounding the squares of light in the windows. He could see Cathy moving about the kitchen in her dressing gown, Gracie on her hip, preparing breakfast.

'Did you get any sleep?' he had asked earlier.

'Yes,' she said. 'Plenty,' but he had felt her slip from their bed during the night, had heard her feet on the floorboards as she went downstairs. He knew she would be on the phone to Martha, her sister, who lived in Castleisland. What Martha made of these late-night phone calls, he didn't know. Martha spoke to him only when matters concerning Cathy or Gracie required it, grudgingly even then, and once a month she posted a cheque for the crèche fees.

He finished the windscreen, leaving the engine running so the car might heat up, and went back into the house. In the hall he removed his wet gloves and put them to dry on the radiator. He could hear his wife and daughter in the kitchen singing 'Incy Wincy Spider'. He watched them through the door, their forms distorted by the patterned glass. Cathy was making porridge. She balanced the wooden spoon on the edge of the pot and shimmied low to the floor, her dressing gown enfolding Gracie like a tent. Gracie screamed and wriggled out, then immediately crawled back in again, pulling the dressing gown tight about her. She poked her face through a gap between buttons and giggled. And as he entered the room, he felt something seep away, like the slow hiss of air from a puncture.

Cathy stepped over her daughter and crossed the kitchen to kiss him on the cheek. There were dark circles under her eyes. She took both his hands in hers and rubbed them gently, frowning at their coldness.

'Is it bad?' she said, inclining her head towards the window.

'Bad enough. You'll need to be careful going to the crèche later.'

'It'll have thawed by then. Do you want coffee?'

He shook his head. 'I'll get some at the office.'

Gracie toddled across the kitchen to reclaim her mother. Cathy scooped her up and she clung, limpet-like, to her neck. Over on the hob, the porridge spluttered in its pot. 'I'll do that,' he said, as he saw Cathy turn. 'You sit down.'

He poured porridge into two bowls and carried them to the table. Cathy lowered Gracie, kicking and protesting, into her high chair and fastened the straps. 'Martha's asked us to go stay with her for a few days,' she said.

He pulled out a chair beside her. 'When?'

'She thought next week might be good. There's a festival on, and a few of the cousins will be around.' She stirred some milk into the porridge, blew gently on a spoonful before putting it to Gracie's lips. He watched the child clamp her mouth shut, contort her small body so she was facing the other direction.

'I don't know,' he said. 'I worry about you being there on your own.'

'We won't be on our own, we'll be with Martha.' She took Gracie's chin in her hand and gently tilted it back towards the spoon. 'You could come down at the weekend, stay for a few days.'

'Did Martha say that?' He knew how Martha felt about him. It was the same way he felt about Martha.

'You know she's always asking us to visit.'

You, he thought, she's always asking you to visit, but just then Gracie released a mouthful of porridge she had quarantined in her cheek. He watched Cathy's hand dart out and catch it on the spoon. Her own porridge was untouched, solidifying into a cold, grey disc.

'Here,' he said, reaching for the spoon. 'Let me feed her, you eat your breakfast,' but she shook her head.

'I can manage,' she said. 'Anyway, you need to get to work.'

He got up from his chair and went over to the window. Outside, light was spreading from the east. The garden was spiky with the stalks of leafless plants and a mound of fermented lawn cuttings leaned, white-capped, against the fence. Gracie's tricycle, left out overnight, was frosted too, snatches of purple breaking through here and there.

It was on a morning like this, white with a hush upon the fields, that they had found the site. They had travelled from Dublin the evening before, the only accommodation a B&B in a village ten miles away, where he had made cautious love to Cathy beneath thin sheets and wiry blankets. She was in the early stages of pregnancy and he had moved inside her with a new restraint, terrified that he might harm the baby, not understanding how very safe his daughter was then, how very protected. The next morning, they met the auctioneer at the field, the farmland all around them in folds of white hills like a bridal gown, jewelled with frost. Small dark birds, feathers puffed against the cold, darted in and out of hedgerows.

'Have you ever seen anything so beautiful?' Cathy had whispered. 'It's like Narnia.'

'Do you think you could live here?' he remembered asking, as they walked behind the auctioneer to where their car was parked in the laneway. 'Yes,' she had answered. 'Yes, I think I could.'

He looked at his watch and saw that it was almost eight. He went over to kiss Cathy and as she lifted her face to his, porridge slid from the spoon and dropped onto the tray of the high chair. Gracie studied it, poked it, traced spirals with her fingers round and round the tray. Cathy just shrugged, mopped up the porridge with the sleeve of her dressing gown. There were mornings when he was unsettled by her eagerness to please him, by the transparency of her efforts to affect happiness. This morning she seemed more relaxed, brighter, her smile as she said goodbye less forced.

But a few minutes later as he sat in his car, key in the ignition, she appeared at the front door. She picked her way across the gravelled driveway in thin, fabric slippers, arms wrapped around herself to fend off the cold.

'You don't have to go to Manchester this month, do you?' she said, as he rolled down the window.

'No,' he said. 'I don't think so.' And he saw relief in her face as she waved him off.

He drove out the gate and down the lane, shattering membranes of ice stretched across the puddles, and turned onto the main road. At Twomey's bridge, a buckled fender and side-panel lay bone-white in the verge, like skeletons along an ancient silk route, a warning to other travellers. His phone sat on the dash. He liked to keep it where he could see it, though he knew it would not ring. Once he joined the river road he was out of coverage until he reached the dual carriageway. The river road was a portal between worlds: his home on one side, the city on the other, and in the middle a no-man's-land of space and time when his wife and daughter were beyond his grasp, unreachable.

Mist rose from the river, ghosted through black and empty trees. The herons that lived along the bank were out in force, balanced on spindly legs. They stood motionless, their long, curved necks thrust forward, as if they too, like the trees and the grass, had been stilled by the frost. The road was rough and uneven. Every spring, the Council sent out men and machines with truckloads of asphalt to lay a new surface. And every winter the river tore it away again, so that, come February, what remained was not so much a road but a dirt track.

His office was in a nineteen-seventies square-fronted building in the city centre. Steps, pock-marked with gum and doused in bleach, lead to a foyer hung with advertisements for various financial products. He saw Cahill, his manager, waiting in the lift lobby and decided to take the stairs. Cahill, he knew, was losing patience. He had considered talking to him but the time had never seemed right and now he thought the time might have passed. Lately he had noticed a change in the way Cahill spoke to him, and if they passed each other in the corridors or in the canteen, Cahill mostly looked away.

His cubicle was on the fourth floor, in a long, rectangular room with floor-to-ceiling glass windows. More glass separated the office space from the stairwell and the staff canteen. He switched on his computer and saw Cahill had included him on an e-mail about the trip to Manchester, scheduled for the following week. He clicked 'reply', typed a couple of sentences and stopped. For a while, he stared at the screen without typing anything, then saved the reply to 'drafts' to finish later.

He made a mug of coffee in the canteen and brought it back to his desk. The woman in the next cubicle raised her head above the partition. 'Cahill was looking for you,' she said, in the sing-song, lisping voice that grated on him, and then she went back to work, synthetic nails scuttling click click across her keyboard. He opened his e-mails and resumed the reply to

Cahill. He read over what he had written, added a word or two, then closed it and started on something else.

At 11.35 a.m. his mobile rang. It was Martha. 'I'm worried,' she said.

He had told Martha time and again that he worked in an open-plan office.

'Hold on,' he said. He got up and went out to the lobby. He pictured Martha on the other end of the phone, her cheeks sucked hollow in annoyance at being kept waiting, tugging at the buttons of her cardigan as if even they had offended her. Between the lifts and the cleaning supplies cupboard was a narrow recessed space. He had discovered that if he pressed close against the wall, he could see his cubicle through the glass, but could not easily be seen himself.

'Okay,' he said. 'Go ahead.'

'Have you noticed anything lately?'

'Nothing worth talking about.'

'That means you've noticed something.'

He wondered how two people who both loved Cathy could dislike each other so very much. 'She doesn't go jogging anymore,' he said. 'But that's mostly down to the weather.'

'Anything else?'

He imagined Martha's fidgeting becoming fiercer, a button popping off her cardigan, rolling across her kitchen floor. He closed his eyes and took a deep breath. He was about to betray his wife. 'She's skipped her meds a couple of times, but only a couple. And she's tired, but then Gracie's been a handful lately.'

There was silence for a moment and then Martha said, 'Gracie isn't at the crèche today.'

'How do you know?'

'I rang the crèche and they told me.'

'You had no business ringing them.'

'I ring all the time,' Martha said. 'Somebody has to. Did you know she forgot to collect Gracie twice last week? They had to phone her when she didn't show.'

'She was probably just late,' he said. 'Late isn't forgetting.'

'She was over an hour late. And yesterday? When they were changing Gracie? Her dress was filthy. Filthy and frayed along one side, and she wasn't even wearing a vest.'

He rested his forehead against the wood of the supplies cupboard, inhaled its smells of bleach and disinfectant. Every small thing had been taken from his wife's possession, laid bare under a harsh and artificial light; every failing paraded before a fairground mirror, magnified and distorted, until even the smallest lapse came to signal catastrophe. 'They told you all that?' he said. 'They had no right. That stuff's private.'

'I don't give a shit about your privacy. Your daughter isn't at the crèche today, you need to start thinking about that.'

Over the top of the cupboard, he saw Cahill weaving through the maze of cubicles heading for his desk. He saw him rest his hands on the back of the empty chair and look around.

'Did you hear me?' Martha said.

'Are they sure she's not at the crèche?'

'Of course they're bloody well sure, they sign the children in, they sign the children out. Your daughter isn't there.'

He could see Cahill bent over the desk, scribbling something. 'I'll ring Cathy now,' he said.

'You think I haven't tried that? I've been ringing this past hour.'

'She might be upstairs, she mightn't have heard the phone. Sometimes she takes her bath while Gracie's at the crèche.'

'I told you,' Martha said, and he pictured her knuckles growing white as her grip tightened on the handset, 'Gracie's not at the crèche.'

'I'll give it ten minutes and try her then.'

'Well, let me know how you get on.'

'I will,' he said. 'And thank you, Martha.' But she had hung up.

He dialled Cathy's mobile but it went to voicemail. The landline also rang out. When he returned to his desk, the woman in the next cubicle appeared again above the partition. 'Cahill,' she said, nodding at a post-it stuck to his computer screen. He peeled it off and read it. He was to bring last month's figures to the lunchtime meeting about Manchester. He crumpled the note into a ball and dropped it in the bin. He tried Cathy's number again. He thought of ringing the crèche, asking if Gracie had arrived in the meantime, but decided against it.

He took the stairs to the third floor to collect some documents and when he got back, he saw he had a missed call from Martha. He looked around the office. Cahill was standing a little way off, talking to one of the IT people. He went back out to the lobby and dialled Martha's number and, when she didn't answer, Cathy's. When there was still no reply, he returned to his desk, took his jacket from the back of his chair, and left the office.

He drove out of the city, past tourists shivering around the war memorial statue, past the park where mothers in hats and scarves chatted over buggies, and took the exit for the dual carriageway. Shortly after he turned onto the river road, Martha rang but the line was patchy, interspersed with bursts of static, and then there was nothing. It was not raining but drops from overhead branches fell in an insistent patter upon the windscreen. Nature had swung on its hinges: the thaw had started and once it had started there was nothing that could stop it. Frost was melting from the trees along the river bank, revealing strips of torn plastic and other debris wound around their trunks in times of flood. There had been an un-silvering: the whiteness had receded, leaving soiled browns, mildewed greens. From a low-lying branch, a plastic bag hung heavy with river water. He remembered a summer at his grandparents' farm as a child, when he had found a bag, a knotted pouch of water, by the edge of a stream. Opening it, he had discovered half a dozen slimy, hairless pups, their eyes tight shut.

There was an incident the previous November that he had kept from Martha. Cathy, he guessed, had kept it from her too, because if Martha knew, Cathy and Gracie would be living in Castleisland now, and he would be living by himself in the house above the river. He had arrived home one evening to find the front door open, leaves blowing about the hall. 'Cathy?' he called, putting down his briefcase. In the kitchen, a bag of flour had been pulled from a cupboard and upended. Gracie was under the table in just a nappy, digging jam from a jar with a fork and smearing it on the floor. She was utterly absorbed, the kitchen quiet apart from the sound of the fork striking the tiles. It was only when she looked up and saw him that she began to bawl. 'Where's Mummy?' he tried, picking her up and going from room to room, but she had only cried louder.

He dressed her in clothes pulled from the laundry basket, and got a torch from under the stairs. Cathy's phone was on top of the kitchen table, her car parked in the driveway. He searched the garden first, quickly, because he did not expect to find Cathy there. The shed when he checked it was padlocked on the outside as usual. Gracie had stopped crying, distracted by the novelty of being outdoors in the dark. She waddled ahead of him, chasing the torch's circle of light, jumping on it, shrieking when it slid from under her feet. He climbed over the ditch into the farm next door, lifting Gracie in after him. He hoisted her onto his shoulders, steadying her with one hand, his other hand sweeping the torch across the shadowy grass as they made their way from field to field.

From the farm, they crossed the road to the stretch of marshy ground beside the river. The countryside at night was a different creature, the soft ground sucking at their shoes, the air thick with midges. As they got closer to the river, he noticed movement ahead, black, lumbering shapes at the edge of the trees. It was a herd of cattle, the white patches of their hides emerging like apparitions from the darkness. They were gathered in a circle, heads dipped low, steam billowing from their noses. 'Moo!' Gracie shouted. 'Moo! moo!' And they stumbled apart to reveal Cathy sitting on a metal feeding trough, the ground all around her pulped muddy by hooves. She was dressed in a skirt, a short-sleeved blouse and slippers, and when he got nearer he saw that her arms and legs were torn by briars and she was bleeding from a cut on her ankle. She looked up at him and then she looked away. Later that night, after he had bathed her and dabbed antiseptic on her cuts, after he had put her to bed and placed Gracie, sleeping, in the crook of her arm, still she wouldn't look at him.


Passing through Lindon's Cross, the car slid and crossed the centre line before he managed to right it again. A heron spread its wings and rose up, came low through the trees, onto the road. It flew so close he feared it might strike the windscreen, but it rose higher and for a moment flew ahead of the car, a silent out-rider, before rising higher again, higher than seemed plausible for such a large bird, and disappearing behind a copse of trees. He touched a hand to his face and realised that he was crying. If he got home and they were safe, he would never leave them again. He would stay with them, he would not go to the office and Cahill could do what he liked. It didn't matter anymore what Cahill thought or didn't think; it was impossible to imagine anything that mattered less than Cahill. They would manage, he would find a way, he would talk to Martha.

When he turned into the driveway, he saw that the ground surrounding the pond had been disturbed. Sods of red clay had been hacked from the lawn, their scalps of white grass run through with blades of green. A number of wooden posts had been brought from the shed and lay in a pile beside a pick axe and a roll of wire mesh left behind by the builder. He stopped the car and got out. The pond itself was a mess of earth and grass, too muddied to allow sight of any fish. Part of the concrete surround was cracked, the ground beside it swampy where the water was slowly seeping away. He looked towards the house and realised that Cathy's car was missing.

He became conscious of the sound of his own breathing, of the ticks and shudders of the settling car engine. He had the sensation of being underwater, of straining against some vast, sucking tide. And then Gracie came barrelling around the corner of the house. She made her way across the lawn, slipping on the wet grass, falling, getting up again. She was wearing a red dress with pink puffy sleeves, the belt flapping around her, and her Tinker Bell sandals. He ran to her and swung her up into his arms, this child he had driven away from this morning, this child he was entrusted to protect from everything and everyone. He clasped her tight, so tight that her chatter was muffled against his shirt. When he lifted his cheek from her hair, he saw Cathy walking up the garden towards them. She was carrying one of Gracie's sandals that had come off when she fell.

'Why are you home?' she said. She was wearing wellington boots and a dress she had bought for a cousin's wedding the year before, a summer dress in flimsy material patterned in blue and yellow parrots. He saw how much looser it hung on her now, how her collarbone pressed sharply against her skin, as if it might break through.

'I forgot a file,' he said.

'What a day for it to happen,' she said, 'with the roads so bad. We didn't even go to the crèche, did we, Gracie? We went to the end of the lane and turned back.'

'Where's your car?'

She was easing the sandal back on her daughter's foot, fastening the strap. 'It's round the back by the shed. I was using it to move the posts, they were too heavy to carry.'

Gracie wriggled out of his arms and went over to the pond. 'Poor fishy,' she said. She knelt on the concrete surround and dipped her arm in the water, wetting the sleeve of her dress to the shoulder. She lifted out a dead, grey fish. Holding it by the tail, she swung it back and forth like a pendulum.

'That damn bird again,' Cathy said. She took the fish from her daughter and laid it down on the grass. 'We saw him through the window and ran out.' She pointed to a gash in the fish's neck, just below the gills. 'He dropped it, but we were too late. Two more are missing. Maybe three.'

'Bad birdie,' Gracie said. 'Bad, bad birdie.' And she stamped her foot.

He wanted to say that it was winter, that the bird was only doing what it always did, what it had to do. That there had never been any hope for those unwitting koi, here in this desolate place where even the river fish struggled to survive. Cathy picked up the axe. 'What are you doing?' he said.

'We're going to keep the fish safe. We're going to build them a cage, like in the zoo. Right, Gracie?' When she brought the axe down, the end lodged in the lawn and she leaned on the handle, worked it like a lever, until another sod broke away. She flipped it over to reveal a tangle of roots on the underside. She was not wearing a coat or even a cardigan and her arms were purple and goose-bumped. So too were Gracie's, he realised. The hem of her dress had trailed in the pond and the wet was soaking upwards.

'Let's leave it a while and go inside,' he said.

Cathy stopped hacking at the lawn. He saw how she was looking at him, confusion in her face, trying to work out if she had displeased him. 'It's okay,' he said. 'It's cold, that's all. We can see about it later.' He took Gracie by the hand and began to walk towards the house, Cathy at his side.

'I rang earlier,' he said, 'I tried a few times.'

'Did you? We've been out here most of the morning, haven't we, Gracie?'

Gracie nodded solemnly at her mother. 'Poor fishy,' she said again.

At the front door, Cathy took off her boots, left them on the step. 'I've been thinking,' she said, 'about the crèche. It's a lot of money for Martha to come up with every month. And we don't really need it anymore, do we? I mean, I'm fine now, I can manage.' She ruffled her daughter's hair. 'We had fun this morning, didn't we? Just Mummy and Gracie?'

'We don't need to decide about the crèche now,' he said. 'We'll talk about it over the weekend.'

Inside the house, Gracie toddled down the hall after her mother. He glanced at his watch, saw that the Manchester meeting was about to start.

'You might as well stay for lunch now that you're here,' Cathy said.

'Sure,' he said. 'Why not?'

Upstairs in their bedroom, he took off his jacket and threw it on the bed. In the ensuite bathroom, he opened the cabinet and took out the box containing Cathy's medication. He counted the pills in their blister pack: exactly the right number, neither too many, nor too few. He splashed water on his face and lay for a while on the bed with his eyes closed. In the inside pocket of his jacket, his phone beeped. He had three messages: a text from the in-house travel department, with booking references for flights and hotels: three nights in Manchester and then — something that had not been mentioned previously — two in Birmingham; a brusque voicemail from Martha, saying she was on her way to check on Cathy, and one from Cahill, asking where the hell he was. He switched off the phone, put it back in his jacket pocket and went downstairs.

In the kitchen, Cathy was frying onions and cubes of bacon in a pan. 'I thought we'd have omelettes,' she said. 'Something quick, so you can get back to the office.' She stood Gracie on a stool beside her and rolled up the child's sleeves. He watched Gracie smash an egg against the edge of the bowl. Half of it slipped over the rim onto the countertop, the rest, studded with fragments of shell, slid into the bowl. Cathy dipped a finger into the raw egg, fished out shards of shell. There was a determined cheerfulness to the way she moved between hob and cupboard, gathering ingredients, a grim precision to the way she chopped another onion. He noticed that she had applied lipstick while he was upstairs, and her hair was brushed. 'Why don't we eat in the dining room for a change?' she said. 'Gracie's going to help me set the table, aren't you, Gracie?' and she lifted the child down from the stool and led her away by the hand.

He stayed by himself in the kitchen, keeping an eye on the omelettes, every so often shaking the pan to stop them catching. Through the window, he saw the frost retreating towards the mountains to the west, remnants of it forming an erratic patchwork on the bonnet of Cathy's car outside the shed. After a few moments, he took the pan off the heat and went to the door of the dining room, a rarely-used room on the other side of the hall.

Cathy was at the end of the table, bent over a large silver tray. It was something they had found in a market in Dublin before they married and it held items of crystal they had received as wedding presents. Cathy picked up a glass, held it to the light, ran a finger along the rim to check for cracks. She polished it with a tea towel, then set it down on the table and took up another. Gracie was arranging red table napkins, folding them and folding them again, pressing them down, protesting as they sprung open when released. Cathy looked up and smiled. 'I thought we'd open a bottle of wine,' she said. 'You could have a glass with your lunch. One glass won't make any difference.'

'I guess not,' he said. Through the dining-room window, he saw Martha's silver Volvo turn into the driveway. It came to a halt by the ruined pond, and he watched as Martha rolled down the window, stared for a while, before continuing on towards the house. 'What a lovely surprise,' Cathy said. 'And she's just in time for lunch.' She left the crystal and went past him into the hall to welcome her sister.

Gracie, finished with the napkins, slid down from her chair. She was looking, not at her father, but about the room, ready for whatever opportunity might next present itself. There was a determined jut to her chin that didn't come from his side of the family, and that always reminded him, not so much of Cathy but of Martha. She headed now, with purpose, towards the tray of crystal. In an instant, she had reached up a small hand and grabbed the corner of a linen napkin on which rested a tall decanter in blue cut-glass. She tugged at the napkin and the decanter, unbalanced, began to topple sideways. 'Gracie!' he heard Martha shout from behind him. But he was watching, as he was always watching, and he was there, just in time to catch it before it fell.

*Jamie O'Connell*

# GRUFFALO

Alice calls. Myles is yet to go down. It's not my turn and my playlist isn't sorted. I open the study door and call up the hallway.

'Myles, get back into bed.'

'No!'

'James, get in here,' Alice says. The argument from the bedroom continues. I take off my headphones and close my laptop.

Myles is on the floor of his room, playing with SpongeBob SquarePants. The curtains are drawn. Alice is sitting on the end of his bed, holding a book. She looks pissed.

'Come in Myles. It's gone eight,' I say.

'I'm not tired.' I drag him towards the bed. Alice tucks his legs in.

'But I don't want to.' He kicks the duvet loose.

'Ah, ah, ah. None of that now,' Alice says. 'What story do you want? There's a few more here.'

Choosing a story distracts him and tears are avoided. I inch back towards the door. As I sit back down at the laptop, I hear them recite lines from *The Gruffalo*, Myles knowing the rhythms and repetitions by heart.


Alice walks into the study. I take off my headphones again.

'How are you getting on?' she asks.

'Fine. He's gone down?'

'Eventually.' She picks at her fingernails. She's dressed in one of my hoodies and grey sweatpants.

'What time is it?' I ask.

'Almost nine.' Alice leans against the desk. I hold her hand, but her fingers don't bend. 'I need a holiday,' she says.

I nod, glancing at my watch.

'I'd better shower.'

Alice's shadow passes the etched glass of the bathroom door. The stairs creak. I gaze at my reflection, run some American Crew though my hair and smile. The television starts downstairs. Alice is probably watching one of those makeover shows. She's always complaining about her weight. I've said I'll pay for a trainer, but she says she has an allergy to wheat or something. I keep myself fit. I go training with the boys on Tuesday and Thursday evenings after I've put Myles to bed.

A shirt is hanging from the bedroom door, which Alice has ironed. She complains about the amount of washing there is. I try not to get annoyed though I work two jobs and she needs to get a grip about what she calls 'busy'.

My alarm goes off at 10 p.m. I put my laptop and cables into the satchel. As I close the study door, I hear Myles's snores. I glance into his room. His duvet has slipped down below his waist, and I creep over and lift it onto his shoulders. His blonde hair is scruffy. He's a handsome devil really, like his father.

I pause at the top of the stairs, listening to a muffled chat-show from below. A part of me resists taking the first step. It reminds me of growing up, when I'd hover in the hallway during dinnertime. I'd listen to the voices through the dining room door, mostly my father's, till my grandmother came looking for me.

Downstairs, I put on my coat and open the living room door.

'Any word from my father today?' I ask.

'He rang earlier,' Alice replies.

'What did he have to say for himself?'

'Nothing. I don't know why he calls.'

I look at her on the couch, legs tucked-up, fluffy slippers and teacup in hand. She looks away from the television and I kiss her goodbye. I tell her I'll be home at three or so.

'Come straight home,' she says.

'I'm wrecked anyway.'

She appears unconvinced. My holiday to Barcelona with the boys kicked it all off. A picture online of me with a Spanish twenty-something on my lap. I said it was just a bit of harmless flirting, that nothing happened, but it's like I've been on proba-tion since June.


A hen party is on the dance floor. They wave up at the DJ box and I smile back. The bride-to-be wears a fake diamond tiara with pink feathers at its base. In the centre of the group, a couple of the women have placed their bags, dancing around them like a totem pole. Now and again a bouncer tells them not to leave bottles on the floor. They apologise but as they buy new rounds of drinks, empty bottles are left resting by their bags.

My mate Sean is standing beside the bar talking to Sarah. Sean is wearing a white shirt, the collar outside his jacket. I often joke that his mother still dresses him. Sarah is sipping a Smirnoff Ice through a straw. Her body and face are turned towards Sean, though her eyes scan the bar. People regularly comment on her eyes; I've heard them called striking, even beautiful. You certainly notice them, though nowadays I think they are too big. Big swivelling eyes in a large skull that barely balances on a skeletal body.

'James,' she reaches in, kissing my cheek. 'How was the set at Electric Picnic? Was it amaaazing? I'm gutted I missed it, but it was Fion's twenty-fifth and then I had that hen for Annette which I couldn't avoid.' She pulls a face.

'The set was unreal.'

'Was Bjork good? I've been dying to see her. I'm raging I missed it.' She drawls over certain words when she speaks, saying 'dying' as if there's literal pain in her chest.

'I missed her,' I say. 'I was playing a set on the other stage.' I look over Sarah's shoulder at Sean. 'How are you bud?'

'I'm good — heading to The Long Island for a few mojitos. Duncan, you know y'man we met at Oxygen, he's having a party at his pad in Blackrock if you're on for it after.'

'I'd say not,' I reply. 'Alice wants me home when I'm done. How'd you get on last night with...'

'I let her in the DJ box and hey presto.' Sean grabs himself. 'Was unreal. Why didn't you stay out after?'

'Alice was on at me.'

'You're whipped.'

'Bloody Barcelona,' I shake my head. Sean goes on to describe the girl and I half listen, having heard a similar story many times before. I glance at Sarah as he talks, not liking that he speaks so openly around her. I shouldn't have done it that one time. Now there's no getting rid of her.

'I'd better keep with the tunes,' I say after Sean finishes. 'There's a bottle of Jameson there if you want to take it with you.' I tap my foot on the mini fridge underneath the decks.

'Nice one.'

'See you later James,' Sarah says. 'We'll see you after?' She gives me one of her big stares.

'Yeah, sure.' I watch them walk towards the bathroom. Sean must have a bag of coke; that's why she's hanging around. I smile. It's a great pleasure to dislike someone.

I play Groove Armada's 'I See You Baby', knowing how its lyrics will affect the crowd. The gamble pays off. The younger girls make their way to the floor. There was a time I'd have scanned for the hottest one, thought about inching over to her and grinding my body into hers, getting hard, kissing her, and then leading her home.

The song ends. The floor thins. I watch the group of girls walk towards the glass doors of the smoking room. I recognise the brunette. I woke up next to her once in a spare bedroom at Sean's house. All I could remember was kissing her, her small lips and darting tongue. I asked for her number then deleted it as I headed home. Her group of friends are no doubt outside, pretending to smoke, asking men for lighters. I've watched their too-straight fingers hold the cigarettes, taking shallow drags and quenching them while there was still an inch of white paper.

'Evening stranger,' a voice says. A hand reaches around my thigh. I pull back, turning to see who it is.

'Marie.'

'So, which one are you eyeing?' she says, wobbling a little on her silver heels. Her smooth hair is cropped shoulder-length. I glance at her body, her toned tanned legs underneath a turquoise cocktail dress. She's forty-five. Money works wonders.

'Where's Peter?' I ask. She pulls a face. She has strong features, hawk-ish, which probably weren't attractive when she was young, but they now preserve her face. Her eyes are pale green. Like Sarah, she's a dangerous woman. Yet her lack of jealousy attracts me, her ability to ask me questions about girls I've been with as we lay together naked. As she said, 'Men are dogs. Put them on a leash and they fight it. Let them off and they always come back'.

'Where's Peter?' I ask again as she steps closer, sipping her white wine. She's not wearing her wedding ring. Alice and I were invited to their house once for dinner and that red-faced fuck spent most the time talking about the paintings he'd bought while Marie tried to play footsie with me under the table. There was one painting in Peter's study that he was particularly proud of; it was of a horse and three hounds standing beside a pile of dead pheasants. He told me he paid thirty grand for it.

'Peter is off in West Cork,' Marie replies. 'Doing God knows what.'

'Who are you here with?'

'Just me,' she says. 'I said to him I'd keep an eye on the place.' She leans over the edge of the stand. I turn away and organise the next song.

'You around after?' she says.

'An hour maybe.'

'You have my number.' I watch her as she walks back to the bar, pausing to talk to the bouncer outside the VIP section. I wonder if she is with him too. Does she have a list of male numbers which she works down if I am unavailable? I wonder if Peter knows, or cares, about it. They're hardly in love, unless this is the type of modern love that's left behind the fairytale.

At 3 a.m. I pack my bags into the BMW boot. The hours alone in the DJ box have brought up doubts. Marie and I have slept together on and off over the years, though recently the amount has increased. She seems more careless, like tonight, approaching me in the club, instead of texting me from the bar and I wonder if this is a sign her detachment is starting to fail.

Driving from the club, inching past the noisy crowds on the footpath, I tell myself this will be the last time I meet her. I pass takeaways full of drunks, eating chips and burgers. The black bins on the streets are overflowing. Beyond City Hall, I turn up the Old Blackrock Road and the streets become hedgerows. I recall the house party Sean mentioned and I text Alice that I'm heading there, feeling guilty as I type.

I open the window and cool air flows in, clearing my head. The crowds are gone and it is silent outside. The ivy on the stone walls gleams like emerald wax. Pulling into the entrance of the Georgian house, I glance at the road, noticing several cars drive past. The front door opens. Marie is in the turquoise dress, still wearing her heels, and she drinks white wine from an oversized glass. I look at her shoes again and think about their heels digging into my skin.

'I thought one of those young ones might have lured you away.' She hands me the wine glass and I take a sip before placing it on the telephone table. We don't go to the sitting room where it normally happens. She never lets me in the master-bed. 'What if he smells us?' Instead, we end up on the rug in the hallway. I enjoy the feel of her body, though there is no soft skin, no plumpness just below her belly button. She keeps her body young by making it hard.

I continue till I hear her moan. I relax, thrusting till I feel that familiar throb. It's sex by numbers, a dance we have mastered, a stroking of egos rather than an animalistic release, usually beginning with her on top, after which I flip her forward, onto her back. Then, eventually I turn her over and she touches herself while I hold her waist and we finish. Then we lie still, tell each other how good it was, and possibly repeat it all again, depending on our individual moods or how much time we have.

Today the one time is enough. I can taste cigarettes on her breath. I look at her line-free forehead, wondering how long I'll have to wait before I can unhook my arm and get dressed. The hallway is cool; she'll get cold soon and want me to leave anyway.

'That was good,' Marie says.

'Yeah, it was.' I stare vacantly at the glass doorway. Overhead, the crystal chandelier scatters the light onto the walls. My fingers touch the condom on the limestone floor at the edge of the mat. I pull my hand away, wishing it would vanish. Now that we've finished, whatever charm there was before is gone. I look back at Marie and smile again, feeling disgust, and wondering if the feeling is mutual.

'You smell funny,' Myles says as I peer in the sitting room door. My T-shirt is coated with cheap antiperspirant that I found in the bathroom at the party. When I arrived, Sean was with Sarah on one of the broken couches, having the face chewed off him. He nudged her and asked what took me so long to get there. She smirked and said something about roadworks, and she'd heard there were detours through Blackrock.

'How's my favourite son?' I ask, wincing at the memory.

'I'm your only son Daddy,' Myles replies, tapping his heels off the leather sofa. But I like saying this to Myles, the way my grandmother used to call me her favourite grandson even though I was the only one.

'Can I get a hug?' I ask. My muscles ache and I realise how tired I am.

'I don't like hugging,' Myles says in a voice that reminds me of Alice. He turns back to the flat screen television. The music for *SpongeBob SquarePants* begins.

'Don't you want these?' I hold up an opaque bag of jellies along with a packet of Monster Munch that I picked up in the corner shop. At the sound of the rustle Myles swings around.

'You're not feeding him sugar, are you James?' Alice calls out from the kitchen. There's a tone. She's still in that bloody mood.

'Of course not,' I reply, handing the wrappers to Myles. I walk up the hallway, avoiding the scattered WWF wrestling figures, like bowling pins mowed down in the hallway. Alice is organising the washing on the kitchen table.

'That's some pile,' I say.

'There always is,' she says, tucking her blonde hair behind her ear. 'You know what time it is?'

'The party went on a bit. Will I put on the kettle?'

'There's sourdough in the bread bin. Christ James, it's nearly nine. You'll miss Myles's match, you know that?'

I say nothing as I put two slices into the toaster and fill the kettle.

'How's Sean?' Alice then asks.

'Sean's good. Nothing new.' I wonder how long the bread will take to toast.

'Isn't it about time he stopped acting like a seventeen-year-old?'

'What's with the twenty questions?'

'You can't keep living like this.'

'Would you give it a break? I've been working half the night.'

'Not till 9 a.m.'

We sit in silence. Alice taps the side of the table with her fingernails. It appears she wants to say something. I think back over the night and a worry creeps up within me. Surely, I didn't miss anything? I checked for perfume, for lipstick.

'Sarah called me last night,' she says finally. 'Out of her head.'

'Oh.' Silence is the only defense. Anything I say will be analysed as she searches for another reason to hate me.

The kettle clicks off.

'You don't want tea?' I ask.

'No.' Alice begins sorting the clothes again. 'She and I talked for ages, you know. Well, she talked rubbish and I listened.'

'You sure you don't want tea?'

'No. I said no.' She starts folding clothes again. My neck feels all twisted and my head is floating somewhere up around the ceiling. I wait for it, for Alice to say, 'I know you weren't at the party' or to mention Marie. But there's nothing, just more silence that goes on for what feels like forever.

Eventually, Alice picks up a school jumper.

'Look at the ice-cream Myles's got on this,' she says, her voice somehow back to normal.

'Alice…' I say.

'Go inside. Spend a bit of time with your son while you can. He's hardly seen you all week.'

Myles is eating a jelly snake. I stand directly in front of the television, trying to get his attention.

'Stop it!' Myles says, yanking his head frantically left and right, trying to see around me. Sitting on the couch, I glance around the room. Toys pile up around the edges, like the line of seaweed on a beach, just beyond the tide.

I pick up a book and glance at the cover. *Aesop's Fables*. It smells of new pages. I look at the image of the fox eyeing the grapes, the grasshopper in the field as the ant is laden with food.

'Don't you like the book?' I ask.

'Yah,' Myles replies, tearing the brightly coloured tail off the snake, eyes fixed on the television.

'What's your favourite story?'

Myles doesn't answer, too interested in his cartoons. I put the book back on the floor, sliding it towards a mound of books and toys.

'Are you going to bed now Daddy?'

'In a minute.'

'Is Mammy cross?'

'She'll be okay.'

Myles continues to eat and kicks his dangling legs off the couch. I close my eyes. I should feel better; it appears I've gotten away with it. Instead, a groan escapes. The groan is louder than I expect. Maybe it's because I've been up for nearly a day and a half, though most likely it's because I've just cheated on Alice again. And she knows it. She just no longer cares.

*Fiona Whyte*

# CIÚNAS

On Christmas morning I climb into the back of the car to set out for Passage West. The ground is sprinkled with beads of frost that wink up at me like a thousand holy stars, and when my father closes the car door I kneel up on the seat to look out the window at the patterns of pirouettes I have traced over the path with my feet. My father sits into the driver's seat, his collar turned up, the peaked hat pulled tight over his head, his breath coming fast and fierce in a scurry of clouds, his nail-bitten fingers tugging the choke and shoving the gearstick as he starts the engine. As we turn the corner at the bottom of our road the car goes into a spin, and I'm thrown from one door to the other. My father curses loudly, but quickly he brings the car back into line, and soon we are phut, phut, phuttering up the steep slope of Shamrock Avenue, me safely back in place; my parcel, neatly wrapped in red and black crepe paper, still intact; my blue satin dress, sewed for me by my mother, still smooth and shiny; my new tights still twinkling white; and surely the creeping stain of damp darkening the toes of my ballet slippers will have faded by the time we reach our destination.

My father mutters something to himself as he leans into the steering wheel and eases the car down Donnybrook Hill onto Church Road. I kneel up again and look out the window. Church Road is a river of people, all swarming in one direction, picking their way over the frost, some walking on the road as there is no room on the path. Everybody goes to Mass. My father is the only person in the whole world, I think, who does not, not even to midnight Mass where the choir sings 'Away in a Manger' and 'Silent Night' and all the other lovely Christmas carols. But Mammy says not to talk about this. He grumbles now, something about right of way and pedestrians who must have some mad death wish hidden beneath their cloaks of piety. I wonder what he means. Everyone I see is wearing a coat — only people in long-ago stories wear cloaks — but I don't think about it for very long because soon we pass beyond the church, under the Bow Wow Bridge, past the Fingerpost, and finally out a straight road that stretches for miles along the river.

Eventually we turn off and come to a long, low wall topped with strange railings that have crosses where there should be spikes. Behind the wall is a fortress of trees, so thick and high that not even the strongest fairy-tale prince could break his way through. The car stutters along and when we reach a gateway it brakes to a halt. The gates, set between two tall pillars, are open. On each pillar stands a stone eagle with wings spread, chest puffed out. They face each other, their hooked beaks pointing proudly upwards to the sky. They are not looking towards each other at all; their eyes are peering down at us instead. I smooth down my dress and check that my tights are still sparkling white. I stretch out my feet and point my toes and hope that the stains on my ballet slippers are barely noticeable. Even my father leans into the steering wheel, his head bent as though he does not want those eagles to see him. But we must have passed the inspection for he starts the engine up again, and slowly we inch up the long driveway that leads to the orphanage of Mount St Joseph at Passage West.

The courtyard in front of the house is full of cars. There is no room for us to park there, so we must drive around to the back. I wait and wait for my father — it's ages before he opens the car door — but eventually he takes my hand, grips it tightly and walks with me around to the front of the house. The house is the largest I have ever seen. Even my father, who is tall and strong, seems small and stooped standing before it. But it's old, dirty yellow, wrinkled with spidery cracks, and there are bald patches where chunks of plaster have fallen off. Black splodges are creeping up the window panes, and paint is peeling away from the frames like bits of dead skin. The whole place looks as if it might come tumbling down any moment now.

My dancing teacher, Miss Cantillon, is standing, arms folded, in the porch. She is wearing a tan-coloured suede coat with a black fur collar and cuffs, a pillar hat that matches the coat, and black high-heeled boots. She manages a shivery smile and a Happy Christmas for my father, who just nods in return. He seems even smaller now, his coat crumpled, his shoulders hunched, and I wish he would stand up straight and fix his collar and wear a tie and go to Mass like other fathers do.

'I'll bring Ruby in,' Miss Cantillon says to him. 'The other parents have already left. They're waiting in the cars over there.'

My father doesn't look at the parents sitting in their cars, or at Miss Cantillon. He looks up at the house and holds my hand tightly. Too tightly. For a moment I think he isn't going to let go, but then suddenly he does. He turns away abruptly and scurries across the driveway without even wishing me good luck.

'Inside quickly,' Miss Cantillon says. 'You're late, you know.'

She marches across the porch, her boots clanking against the cracked tiles, and I follow her through the yawning door into the big house.

Inside is bedlam. Shrieking, laughing, roaring. A blizzard of boys chasing about a large hall, half-chewed Peggy's Legs and liquorice sticks in their fists. They push and shove and knock each other over, laughing all the harder when someone goes down. They dash about the hall as if it is a playground, their screams of laughter ringing out so loud it hurts my ears. I wait for someone to take charge, but no one does; not the nuns huddled in the corner next to the spindly Christmas tree; not the man at the top of the huge winding staircase, leaning against the banister, his chin jutting upwards as if he is one of those old eagles; not even the tall nun in the middle of the hall who is standing straight, her hands tucked into her sleeves, watching everything, her face frozen into a smile like a doll's.

Miss Cantillon goes to talk to the nuns. I stand next to the doorway, pressed up against the wall, clutching my parcel. The wall is cold and clammy; its chill creeps into my skin. A buzzing tingling feeling ripples through my head. I watch the running, tripping feet of the orphans. Not one is quietly sitting on the bottom step of the stairs or gazing out the window, waiting for a new Mammy and Daddy to come and get them. It's not like in my storybooks at all. Suddenly I am scared of this big old house. There's a smell here. It reminds me of the time we found a dead rat in the cupboard under the sink and Mammy screamed and screamed and we had to wait for my father to come home from work to get it out.

Eventually the tall nun — the head nun, I think — comes over to me. 'This way,' she says. She curls her forefinger in that way that teachers do and leads me to a large room off the hall. Dozens of classroom chairs are laid out in rows in front of a low platform made from old wooden crates. On the wall behind the platform is a cardboard sign written in red and black crayon. *Welcome, Miss Moira Jane Cantillon's School of Dance.* The other dancers from my class are crowded around an empty fireplace. My friends Maeve and Claire are there, wearing their toy soldier outfits — boys' black pants and red T-shirts with two strips of white crepe paper pasted in an X across the front. No one has a costume even half as lovely as my blue dress. I want to go over to them but the nun catches my arm. 'You may leave your present there,' she says, pointing to a table strewn with scraps of tinsel, wrapping paper and sweet wrappers just inside the door.

In my parcel is a facecloth, a round cake of Yardley's Lavender Soap, a packet of magic markers, a Trebor liquorice sherbet, a Curly Wurly, a twopenny lollipop and a packet of Rowntree Love Hearts. I picked out the Love Hearts especially. Suddenly a swarm of children descends. Hands snatching, tugging, hitting. Scraps of flimsy crepe paper flying about like sparks and ash. A red-haired orphan is picking open the wrapper on the Love Hearts when it is grabbed from him by another boy; the Curly Wurly is held in a tug of war; the sherbet almost falls to the floor but is caught by a boy who dives to catch it, rolls on the ground, then jumps up quickly and runs off.

'Now, now,' the nun says, but the children disappear in a gust of flakes of red and black, while she stares after them, the doll smile still tight on her face. I run to join my friends and we huddle together tightly.

'Why are they so rude?' Claire says. 'They didn't even say thank you! And why are there so many of them?'

The tingling in my in my head grows stronger, like an itch I can't reach. So many orphans. So many children whose parents are dead, killed in car crashes, like in the books. Like my father's parents. But that's another thing Mammy says not to talk about.

The red-haired boy returns. He rifles through the scraps on the table and finds the cake of Yardley soap. His eyes widen, and he holds the cake very close to his chest as he rips the tissue wrapping away. He sniffs at his prize, turns it over in his hands and stares at it as if there has been some terrible mistake. He mutters something, but not quietly enough. I feel the heat rush into my cheeks.

'Fuck's sake!'

He throws the soap to the ground and runs off.

'Jack!' the nun calls, grim-lipped now. 'Jack!' She strides from the room without picking up the soap.

Miss Cantillon comes in, finally. She ushers us onto the stage and tells us to take up our positions. Outside someone blows a whistle. It pierces through the noise.

'Ciúnas! Líne! CIÚNAS!'

The shouting and laughing dies away, and a few moments later the orphans straggle into the room. 'Suígí síos anois', the head nun says. Her voice is loud and clear, and also sweet, as if it has been pasted in sugar. 'Anois!' she says, more loudly and still more sweetly, and she fixes her eyes on a pair of boys who seem not to understand. Another nun appears, prods them in the arm and motions to them to sit down. Lastly, the man on the staircase comes in. He is tall and dressed very smartly with a crisp white shirt, a red bowtie and a blazer just like the one Maeve's father wears when he goes to work in the bank. He leans against the doorframe, arms folded, watching the boys as they fidget and shuffle in their seats, nudging each other and chewing their sweets.

I stand at the centre of the stage, feet in first position, head bent, shoulders bent, arms stiff, elbows out. Miss Cantillon snaps the tape into the cassette recorder. The music begins. The trumpets sound the opening notes, pure and bright. The violins answer. A sudden burst of sunlight streams through the window. My satin dress shines blue as the sky, my tights sparkle white as the frost, and after months of practising I am here at last, centre stage in the sun, ready to perform my solo dance for the poor orphans.

The soldiers march in a circle about me as they wait for the magic moment of midnight when the doll will come to life. Ticktock goes the music, ticktock. Bong. I open my eyes. Bong, bong. Forward I go, four stiff mechanical steps. The soldiers fall back. Keep the shoulders forward, head bent. Bong. Stop. Move the right arm, one, two, three stiff clockwork movements. Bong, bong. Repeat with the left. Bong. Relax the arms. *Bras bas*. Stretch them out, slowly, elegantly, in time to the music.

Now point the toes, no longer a clumsy, mechanical windup toy, but a beautiful ballerina. I shape my arms, bring the palms forward, relax the fingers. Then *plié*, rise. Again. *Plié*, rise. Now *piqué*. Now pirouette. Once. Twice. In time to the music. Again. Stay in time. Listen to the music.

But it's difficult to hear the music. A murmur has started, bubbling up like a stream, rising to the sound of a waterfall. Shh, I hear someone, shh. But the orphans don't shh. They are giggling again, shuffling, chatting. The red-haired boy jumps out of his seat and pretends to dance. He spreads his arms.

'Jack!' someone hisses. Loudly.

I pay no heed. I am at the front of the stage. I lean on the front of my right foot and spin into another pirouette, elegant, graceful. But the red-haired boy spins too. He spins around. His arm knocks against my leg. Hard. And down, down I fall. The thump that booms out like a drum is me as I hit the floor.


Afterwards is a rush of goodbyes. Parents spill into the hallway to collect their children and call out cheery thank yous and Happy Christmasses as they take them by the hand and steer them through the front door. Maeve and Claire disappear and I am left alone. The draught from the open door is vicious and it blows the sweet wrappers across the floor. I rub my fingers along my satin dress and I see that it is scuffed. There is a hole in one of the knees of my tights. The stains on my ballet slippers seem bigger and darker. And my head aches. Where is my father? I want him to come. Now. I want to tell him about the horrible red-haired boy and the ungrateful orphans. I want him to take me home.

Cars start up outside, engines snorting and growling.

Gradually the noise patters away. Then an aeroplane sound. Inside. It's the red-haired boy racing around the hall, hrum-hrumming as he leaps into the air and kerpowing as he crashes to the floor.

'Jack! Enough now!'

The sugar has melted away from the head nun's voice. Her face is apple-red. The man with the bowtie is sidling over, a pipe dangling from the side of his mouth.

'Don't be worrying yourself, Sister. Too much sweets is all that's wrong. I'll sort him out for you. He'll be good for me. Won't you, Jack?'

He catches the boy by the hand, and pulls him into his side. Suddenly Jack isn't wild anymore. He hangs his head, looks sullenly at the ground. He rubs his feet against the floor as if stamping out a cigarette. His shoes are scuffed and the sole is peeling back from the toe. When the nun's back is turned he tugs away from the man, but the man pulls him back in.

'Upstairs to the office with you, Jack,' he says. 'Ciúnas now.'

Jack doesn't look at him. He looks over at me and stares. A hard, bitter stare. I want to look away from him, but I cannot. He is staring at me, and I am staring back. I see his chocolate-stained mouth, his grubby cheeks and dirty nose, and his dark, bitter eyes, scowling, howling.

A bang on the door and footsteps hurrying towards me. My father's face is red, his eyes are red, and he is breathing fast. He sweeps me up in his arms and holds me tight. 'I was waiting for you out the back,' he says. His voice is funny, muffled, as if he has a bad cold. 'Let's go,' he says. 'We need to go.' I am much too old to be carried, but I nestle into his neck anyway as he kisses the top of my head. His breath smells of something sour and stinging — the whiskey Mammy pours on the Christmas cake. He hugs me even more tightly and carries me to the door, snuffling and sniffling. I look over his shoulder up at Jack who has reached the top of the stairs. Jack's head is bent, and the man is stroking the back of his neck, the way my father sometimes does to Mammy. Jack rubs something from his eyes, and I realise that he is crying too.

Daddy carries me to the car. He puts me in the back seat and makes a blanket for me with his coat. 'We'll soon have you warmed up,' he says, still snuffling. 'You can tell Mammy about your dance when we get home.' He wipes his face with his sleeve, sees me looking at his stained cheeks. 'It's just the cold,' he says. 'Just the cold. No need to mention it to Mammy, alright?'

He steers the car down the driveway, towards the eagles, still perched on their pillars, still staring at us. He mutters something as we pass through the gateway. 'The gates of hell,' I think he says. He is still muttering as we drive home.

*Martina Evans*

# KNOCK

*Coughlin... helped to keep all in good humour, and his droll sayings were repeated. He had been billeted in a house which had a reputation for being stingy. One morning the woman of the house asked him how he liked his eggs boiled. 'With a couple of others, ma'am,' he replied.*

— Ernie O'Malley, IRA Commander

No one wanted Ireland free more than myself, don't I remember as a child, my mother grabbing hold of us, making us lie down on the floor so we wouldn't be seen by the landlord out for his day with the ducks in the bog and his gun broken across his arm, looking to quench his thirst with a glass of milk. *I say! Very refreshing indeed* and a big slick of cream stuck to his old moustache. Ah those days are gone, thanks be to God, old Pym would be afraid of his life to come up to

Knock in his plus fours now. That's what I was thinking this morning and how great it was to be able to open the bottom half of the door and stand out on the flags in my sack apron, the tongues of my boots hanging open. A brown cake baking in the bastable and the air tasting like lemonade. The sun going across my shoulders like a warm coat as I walked over to the henhouse with Blackie the cat pressing up against me. And I was walking out again with six hot white eggs in my big sack pockets, thinking of the breakfast I was going to have with Diarmuid when didn't I see a crowd of them coming round the corner with the old rifles upon their shoulders, singing 'Oro Se De Bheath Abhaile' and my stomach sank to the tongues of my boots. Coughlin, the first as usual, to smell the brown cake. It wasn't that I wasn't wishing them the best of luck the whole time and you might think I'd be worried if we were caught out by the Tans and burned to the ground and I am not saying I wasn't always worried about that too, but to have to turn around and serve a crowd of men and make up beds and to have to pretend to be laughing away at their jokes. Oh God Almighty, I was pure sick of them all then. I remember the first time they came and I was given a pile of dirty socks and Diarmuid handing the pile to me like it was a chalice and I, like a mope, thinking it was some kind of an honour to be scraping the mud off them and when they were dry the next day, didn't I darn the lot of them like an even bigger mope. But this morning, anyway, I hid a couple of the eggs for ourselves and got a big pot of porridge going. 'Twas when Coughlin made his smart remark that I had to walk over to the fire because I thought I was going to cry and the only thing that cured me, as I was looking down into the bubbling oatmeal, was when I remembered being told how the waiters above in the Victoria Hotel in Cork might spit into the soup of a customer if they took a turn against him. And I am still smiling now through my stupid old tears, sitting by the well in the dark, thinking of what I've just put between our sheets after my old mope, Diarmuid gave our bed away to Coughlin for the night. Diarmuid, insisting, right go wrong, that it was a great honour and that nothing else would please me.

*Marie Gethins*


# NOAH SHOULD HAVE READ COMICS

Things changed when a steel currach appeared in the middle of our roundabout. Passage West's Tidy Towns Committee had talked about replacing the boxwood topiary yacht for ages, but an industrial-strength sculpture surprised everybody. 'It's an omen,' my brother Colm said. (He's really into dystopian.) A week later he started hauling planks onto the garage roof and I found out that itch between my toes wasn't Athlete's Foot.

We're not what you'd call a nautical family. Yeah ok, our great-grandad is a legend in the salmon-poaching community. There was talk of a memorial for him by the old bridge outflow, but that's as far as it went. Dad won't even use the river ferry. When I asked if I could take sailing lessons in Monkstown, he said, 'It's *terra firma* for this family.' Of course, Colm figured a way around it. He helped last summer with sport-fishing cruises. Me? Swimming lessons in an over-chlorinated hotel pool is the most aquatic I've ever been.

I kind of get why the neighbours went all strange when they saw Colm building a boat on our garage roof. At the end of a cul-de-sac, there aren't a lot of excuses to stand around our house. First, it was a few old lads using a shortcut on their way to the Men's Shed. An interest in woodworking and all that. Colm nodded to them, but when he didn't stop for a chat, they came up with their own theories.

'What do you reckon — a garden bench? Table? A gazebo for his mam?'

'Makes no sense, your man working outside, what with this weather.'

'He needs to work in the open air, all that sawdust.'

'Saw-mush, more like.'

Word spread. It became a thing. Standing in lashing rain, huddled under golf umbrellas, the lot of them shouting tips. My brother just went about his business: sanding, hammering, checking the spirit level. Colm wore wellies and wet gear that Dad got off some county council worker. HighVis-teen with CCC on his back creating the Big Mystery. If the neighbours had asked, Mom would have told them it was an art project for the Leaving. Mom and Dad swallowed Colm's line about it being too big 'an installation' for the art room. Unbelievable. Of course, our parents were a bit distracted by The Tenerife Apartment Plan. Mom started drawing rain clouds on the kitchen calendar back in September, moaning every time there was a flood warning on the Rochestown Road. 'It's 26°C and dry in Santa Cruz!' OMG. The two of them worked every extra shift going, stashed away cash. Colm and I ate a lot of fish finger sandwiches. He grilled. I assembled.

'This week I'm sanding the afterbody along the apron.'

'Uhuh.' I squeezed ketchup onto slices of bread. Poured two glasses of Coke.

'Battening the seams, that will be important, with what's coming.'

'Uhuh.'

Colm forked fish fingers onto half of the bread. I closed the sandwiches and pressed each one until red oozed onto the crusts.

'Muireann, you listening?' Colm put the grill pan into the sink, turned on a tap. It hissed at the first drops before the gurgle drowned its heat. 'Got to get ready.'

'You've been watching *The Hunger Games* again.' I handed him a plate.

'I'm serious.'

Colm pulled a blue notebook out of his backpack.

'Look,' he said.

He'd always been kind of obsessed about the weather, but this was something else. He'd recorded rainfall for the past two years. He'd even made monthly trend graphs, printed them out, and pasted them in there. He had three meteorological apps downloaded onto his phone and wrote data comparisons into the notebook.

'Mr Roberts, your maths teacher, would be proud,' I told him. Condensation ran off my glass, dripped onto the table. I made an air circle with my finger above a group of five drops. They wriggled across the table and flowed together. Colm opened a window, pointed to the bruised sky.

'It's coming, Muireann. The Big One,' he said.

'It smells like chlorine.'

'Ozone... storm on the way... cumulonimbus clouds.'

My feet started itching like mad. I pushed the last of my sandwich into my mouth and went to my room.

Socks off, I did a careful check, even though I knew what I'd see. The skin flaps had been creeping up between each toe, bit by bit. I googled 'webbed toes'. It was a genetic problem that affected babies, not something that happened when you were thirteen. Reading about the surgery options killed any plan to visit a GP. A banner in Ms O'Shea's classroom said *Embrace your Uniqueness*, so over the next two months I ordered Aquawoman comics online, started doodling Queen Marella of Atlantis during class and wondered when my superpowers would kick in.

Colm finished his boat. I had to admit — though not to him — it was hatchet. The inside all shiny with varnish, a hold in the front (ok, bow) for stuff, two bench seats. He painted the outside pea-green. Wouldn't be my choice, but Colm called it 'good camouflage'. He covered it with a tarp and tied a rope to a corner of the roof. Dad gave him money for oars and all. He said to Colm, 'We'll have to give it a test.' As if Dad would get into a boat. As if Dad was ever around more than five minutes.

Colm decided to have one of his disaster movie fests. *Waterworld, The Day After Tomorrow, Poseidon, The Impossible, Tidal Wave, The Perfect Storm.* He scribbled into his notebook while I ate nuked popcorn. Without Colm on the roof, the umbrella gang didn't know what to do with themselves. A few stomped around the front garden, sinking in Mom's flowerbed. They pushed dripping noses against our sitting room window, eyeballed us. The rain got heavier and after a couple of nights they drifted away, one by one.

'Shouldn't you be studying for the Leaving?' I hated to sound like a parent, but somebody had to ask.

'This is way more important,' said Colm.

He added bottled water, multi-vitamins, and protein bars to the weekly grocery list, telling Mom they were for the Leaving. On the estate green, puddles got bigger and bigger until it became one massive pond. A council truck dropped off sandbags to block front doors, but fingers of water went around them and seeped across our entrance hall. I rolled towels, squashed them against the metal rain deflector. Finished, I went into the sitting room and looked out. Tiny waves lapped at the sill, each lit by a sliver of street light. The sky turned white then black. A thunder boom rattled the window. Monster drops made thousands of crowns. I went back into the hall.

A slick had crept out from under the towels, moved across the tiles. I concentrated, waved my hands in the air, motioned it backwards. Maybe I needed a catchphrase. 'SHAZAM.' Did the water tremble? My toes began to ache. 'EXCELSIOR.'

'What are you doing?' Colm frowned.

'Nothing.'

'Stop feckin around. We need to move the small stuff upstairs.'

RTÉ called it a 'heavy storm' in the morning, a 'major storm' by nine o'clock. Mom rang. She got a text to say schools were closed for the rest of the week, the Rochestown Road impassable. She and Dad stayed on at work. The drops sounded like hail against the windows. I put in earbuds, set the volume loud. I was asleep when Colm shook my shoulder. He said to get my backpack ready. I slipped in the best comics, along with his list of essentials, exchanged jeans and a t-shirt for a dark green swimsuit and leggings. I dug out a sparkly gold top and covered it with a fleece.

Colm waited on the landing. I followed him into Mom and Dad's bedroom. He opened the en suite window. We squeezed out onto the garage roof, raced to his tarp-covered boat, ducked inside. Rain smacked against the plastic. I sniffed: water, stone, mud. Colm nodded. 'Petrichor, that's what the scientists call that smell.' He checked his phone. I held the torch while he added stats to long columns in his notebook.

'Rising fast, it won't be long.'

Colm gave me a quick hug. 'Don't worry. I've got a plan to keep us safe,' he said.

'I've got one too.'

I took out an Aquawoman comic, lit a panel with the torch beam. Queen Marella stood in her green and gold bodysuit, hair streaming behind her, arms straight with her fingers splayed. Water swirled around her, knocking books off shelves as people dove for cover. The caption underneath read: *Hydrokinesis — the power to control water.*

Colm smiled and shook his head. I pulled off the fleece, then runners and socks, fanned out tingling toes. I shone the torch onto my feet.

'See,' I said.

Colm touched the skin between each toe. 'What the…'

I rolled the tarp back off the bow. Puddles dotted the uneven garage roof. I stood, braced each leg against the boat sides. A few shoulder rolls and finger flexes, I smoothed my gold top and looked back at Colm.

'Watch.'

*Donal Moloney*

# WHERE AS A CHILD I'D BEEN

Somewhere past Claremorris, a rattling started up under the bonnet. It quickly progressed into a clanking, and a few miles down the road the car began to judder.

It gave me a kind of grim satisfaction. For years, the engine management light had been going on and then off again, always threatening to make me fail the NCT. I'd been to three garages and the main Peugeot dealership, and nobody could find the fault. I'd even replaced the battery long before it was due.

And now, finally, something real had happened! It was better on balance, I felt, to have an expensive problem than to be gaslit by a dashboard display.

I was on the downslope of a big hill, so I put the car in neutral and let gravity do its work. On the near fringe of a town whose name I've forgotten, there was a sign for a garage in one hundred metres. When I got closer, all I could see was a bricked-up petrol station with two rusted pumps. But just in time, I spied a handwritten sign nailed to a wall, which pointed me round the back.

I wrenched the steering wheel and changed into first. It was a steep climb up the forecourt of the disused petrol station to the yard behind, and my car made such a noisy entrance that birds scattered in all directions and a cat fled in panic.

A tall grey-haired man in overalls came out to greet me.

I got out and explained what was up.

He did not reply at first, but then he held his hand out for the key and said: 'Let's have a look at her.'

His workshop was a little shed with a corrugated iron roof. He reversed a Toyota Yaris out so that he could fit my Peugeot in.

He opened the bonnet and frowned. Then, folding his arms, he said: 'We'll let her cool off.'

'Is there anywhere I can get a coffee or something?' I asked.

His expression showed no sign of having heard me, so I repeated the question.

He waved his arm in a southerly direction. 'Next pub is a mile that way. But it won't be open at this hour.'

After a while, he put his head under the bonnet and got to work. It was a pleasant April morning. As I paced around the yard in the gentle sunshine, the anger that had washed over me began to slowly evaporate along with the puddles in the cracked concrete.


At around 5 o'clock that Saturday morning, by an unfortunate coincidence, my mother-in-law had come downstairs to find me weeping at the kitchen table. She winced when she saw me.

Although I knew she sometimes ghosted around the house at night, that never used to concern me. Before my wife Fiona got sick, I had the soundest sleep. No, that's not quite accurate. When Fiona was beside me in the bed, I slept. On the few occasions one of us was away for the night, I would wake up in the middle of the night and worry about things.

Now that Fiona was gone, the cord connecting me to sleep was severed. And that meant I was at risk of encroaching on my mother-in-law's wee-hour prowlings.

'Good morning,' I said, wiping my eyes.

'I'm not dealing with maudlin bullshit at this hour,' she said and flung open the back door. I could hear her furiously grinding the wheel on her lighter before she got a flame.

After her smoke, she came back in and stood over me. Primly wrapping her dressing gown tight around her, as if I was a stranger who had not seen her in her nightdress at all hours of the morning, afternoon and evening, she said: 'I know what it's like to cry like that.'

'Really?' I asked.

'Yeah, really. I cried like that for a month when my beautiful girl settled for you.'

I laughed and thought how Fiona would get a kick out of that. I'd tell her and she'd give her mother hell. And then I remembered Fiona was dead.

That changed everything. With that release valve closed, the anger rose inside me.

I grabbed my wallet and my keys and went. Because I had nowhere to go, I decided to go home. Far away from Donegal and all its drama, back to where *my people* had been.

I could have taken Fiona's Nissan Leaf for the trip. But I just wanted to go and burn some fuel, and not worry about finding chargers along the way.

I got breakfast in Tobercurry and petrol in Claremorris. As I stewed over the insult, the question formed in my mind: Why should I share a house with a woman who despises me?

Fiona had taken her mother into our house out of a sense of duty. Our daughter Niamh had moved to Singapore the year before, so her room was empty. 'How can I refuse her if we have the space?' Fiona pleaded.

'Every time you meet her, she gets under your skin,' I reminded her.

'She's family!' was the emphatic reply.

Not that we were the old lady's first choice. She had been evicted by two enraged daughters-in-law before she ever got to us. A third had refused point-blank to take her in and threatened divorce.

The merry-go-round had started when a crack formed in the front wall of the little seaside house she had bought after Fiona's father died. She was convinced it was mica damage and felt unsafe living there. At the same time, she refused to get the house assessed for mica, even when Fiona and her brothers offered to pay for the test. We all had our doubts, to be sure.

In the first days and weeks after Fiona's death, her brothers and their wives were exceptionally nice to me, hugging me and telling me what a great man I was to look after the poor grieving woman. But it struck me, with the month's mind only next Thursday, that I'd seen a lot less of them lately.

Around the perimeter of the yard, there were a few cars draped in tarpaulins. Behind them was a stone wall, which separated the yard from a scrubby field. Choked with ragweed, it contained two scrawny horses. Beyond that, there was a soccer pitch. A schoolgirls' match was on, with a good crowd watching. Occasionally the wind carried the blast of a whistle or the urgings of a coach over to me.

The sun went behind a big cloud and the temperature dropped. In my haste this morning, I'd forgotten to bring a jacket. I just kept walking in circles, watching the match in a distracted way, observing the weeds on the grass verge beneath the stone wall, and wondering what kind of cars were under the covers.

In the absence of new things to look at, my attention fixed on the wing mirrors poking out from under the tarpaulins. There were thick spider webs all over them. I'd never seen webs as thick and densely spun. There was a ropiness to the way they bounced in the wind, and they held fat drops of water and big spindly insects.

A wind came through the yard, making me shiver. The match was over and the crowd was dispersing. The spider webs flapped heavily but did not break.

The mechanic emerged from his workshop. His movements were stiff. 'The timing chain is broken,' he said. 'And some of the pistons and valves are damaged.'

'Do you have the parts?' I asked.

He took so long to answer that I wondered if he'd heard me. Eventually he shook his head. Studying his face, I realised he was much older than I'd originally assumed. He was long past retirement age.

I blurted out: 'I hate that car. That car doesn't deserve to be fixed.'

I didn't know I hated the car before, but there it was — out of my own mouth.

'I want a car without an engine warning light,' I said.

The mechanic scratched his cheek. 'I might have something for you.'

He walked over to one of the cars in the yard. He lifted off the stones holding down the tarp on one side, while I did the same on the other. When he grasped the tarp to pull it off, I realised that his middle and ring fingers were bent and that he couldn't close his fist properly on the material. I grabbed the tarp from the other side and helped him lift it off.

It was a silver Lancia Thema saloon, a car that used to be on the roads when I was a teenager. There was green mould around the windows and mud on the body, but otherwise it looked in reasonable nick. As the mechanic went back to his workshop to fetch the key, I gazed through the driver's window at the brown suede upholstery, the wooden trims, and all the mechanical levers, buttons and switches.

'I restored her myself,' said the mechanic. 'Took her for a spin last week just for the pleasure of it. She's running beautifully. All she needs is a clean.'

'Is she roadworthy?' I asked.

'She sure is,' he replied.

Holding his two crooked fingers out of the way, he opened the driver's door with the key held between thumb and index finger.

I sat inside for all of two seconds before saying: 'Yes, please.'

He wanted two grand on top of my Peugeot. I'm sure it was a bad deal, but what did it matter? Who would I be impressing with my negotiation skills? Insisting on cash, he took me in the Lancia to the AIB in Tuam. 'Feel that!' he exclaimed every time he went up a gear.

As we filled out the paperwork back at the garage, he gave me a few pointers on ownership of a classic vehicle. He'd become more expansive ever since he'd unveiled the Lancia.

Finally, he gave the car a hose and a hoover, and by one in the afternoon I was on the road again.

I thought of taking a selfie with the Lancia and sending it to Niamh. But she might misinterpret the situation, think I was off enjoying myself with Fiona not a month in the ground.

Outside of Athenry, the gardaí were diverting traffic. As the diversion took me a long way inland, I decided to drive on to Athlone and take the road south from there.

I had a chicken sandwich and a coffee at a petrol station near Birr.

It was in County Limerick or maybe Tipp that the radio came on. There was a blast of static and then a woman with a thick accent talking like the clappers. I marvelled at how fast she spoke. You get used to the drawl in Donegal, the leisurely vowels.

She was talking about singing sisters whose name I didn't catch, and then she played a request for a couple from Aherlow.

After a gentle intro, a man sang a song about returning to his hometown. Just a simple song, it couldn't help but move me on a day like today.

The voice sounded familiar. My mother-in-law had country music playing in the kitchen all day long. I couldn't say I liked it or didn't like it, but it was the music I heard most often.

'Lovely singing there. Nobody could have sung it better. That's 'In the Middle of Nowhere' sung by Charley Pride and written by the late, great Liz Anderson. Who was a big influence on…'

The presenter continued at a clip that would put a horse racing commentator to shame. It went on like that — song and informative rapid-fire intro, song and rapid-fire intro, the occasional request — until the station disappeared with a hiss and I cruised the lonely roads into Bweeng, County Cork.

The old house was in an awful state. There were slices of masonry missing from the garden wall. The box hedge was a sprawling mess. Strewn around the front garden were an upturned wheelbarrow, a trailer, a mattress with the foam sticking out, a big lump of concrete.

There was no sign of the rose bushes Mammy had tended until she broke her hip. Weeds sprouted out of the guttering, and paint was peeling off the window frames. I strained to see if the old pear tree was standing out the back, but the overgrown hedge blocked my view.

I don't know who bought the house when Daddy died. My siblings looked after all that. After Daddy went, my thoughts turned away from Bweeng and I hadn't been back since.

As discreetly as I could, I took a photo and sent it to Niamh. It would be evening in Singapore. I tried not to contact her too often, as I knew she'd be working long hours to make up for the time she took off for Fiona's funeral. But at the end of the day, I'd rather be annoying than cold.

I got back in the car and drove the few hundred yards to St Columba's. The car park was empty and there was nobody around. Although the façade was a bit grimy, the handsome little church looked as homely as ever.

The main door and the sacristy door were closed when I tried them. I wondered if the parish priest was still alive. What was his name? I could see his jet-black hair and his twinkly eyes. I could remember the way he would take his glasses off and squint at me as I brought over the water and the wine. I could remember the wedding where the groom had neglected to slip the altar boys some money, and how the priest had given us ten pounds each out of his own pocket. Father... Father... no, the name wouldn't come.

In the little graveyard beside the church, I found Mammy and Daddy's grave. There were no flowers or candles or anything by the headstone. My sister Patricia was living in Mallow and I thought she would have looked after it. But she had troubles enough with her husband, I suppose, so I couldn't blame her.

With six children, you'd think you'd have somebody to tend your grave. But there are not many jobs in Bweeng, that's for sure, and time had scattered us far and wide: Mallow, Tralee, Dublin, Donegal, Swansea and California.

Anyway, never mind other people. I should have bought flowers on the way. And if I hadn't been so self-absorbed all day, I would have.

It occurred to me that there might be wildflowers in the park I could pick for the grave. The sun was out and there was a gentle breeze, so I went there on foot. Passing through the village centre, I noticed some new things — a painted wagon wheel fixed to a rock, a flat metal sculpture of a man shoeing a horse, some signs for stray tourists showing local walks—but mostly everything was just as it had been — the little shack that served as a bus stop, the little post office with the post box outside.

When I reached the park, my phone bleeped with a message from Niamh.

'???'

'Where I grew up,' I wrote back.

'You all fit in there?!' replied Niamh.

I'd never planned it this way, of course. Who would want their daughter to have only the faintest idea where they were from? It's not that far from Donegal if you drive straight through. But Fiona's family was... well, difficult is probably fair... and always seemed to be in crisis. It got so bad at times that I didn't like leaving Fiona and Niamh there alone. So either all three of us would make the trip south, or else we'd stay in Donegal.

It's just the way of the world — the unbalanced people get all the attention. That being said, when we did drive down to Bweeng — the last time as a trio when Niamh was about four, before her carsickness grew severe — the red carpet wasn't exactly laid out for us. I was the second youngest in our family and Mammy and Daddy already had seven grandchildren by the time Niamh was born. Our arrival from the far northwest generated little excitement. That, too, is often the way of the world.

The park was much as I remembered it, although smaller. In the shade of some alder trees, I found violets and primroses, bluebells and celandines. I plucked some of each and bound them together with the fresh shoots of a hawthorn bush.

Two boys were out on the pitch, kicking a football back and forth, just like I used to do with my friend Michael until his family upped and went to Australia. Living in a village and kicking a ball back and forth on a lonely field — that's a form of eternity.

When I completed my walk of the park, there were three women standing outside the community centre. I didn't recognise them and they didn't pay me any mind.

On my way back through the village, a man stopped me. He was in his seventies, at a guess, and carried a cane.

'Tommy, is it? It can't be!'

'Tommy was my brother,' I explained. 'I'm—'

'Tommy was some hurler.'

'By all accounts, yes. I remember all his trophies on the mantelpiece.'

Tommy was the eldest. He'd left home already by the time I'd started school.

'Where is he now?' the man asked.

'Tralee.'

The man spat on the ground. 'What do they know about hurling?'

I should have recognised this man, surely? Was he a coach for Kilshannig in those days? Or did he have a son who played on a team with Tommy? I'd spent eighteen years in this village and had lived and breathed the life of the place — the only life I knew. How could I not know this man?

When I'd laid my hand-picked bouquet down at the grave and said a prayer, I took a stroll to my old primary school. It had been extended since my day and looked spick and span. A chorus of tin whistles came out of an open window. I seemed to remember being happy here, at this school, but I couldn't remember a single thing that happened during my time here, except... yes, except that I was in a fight once and got sent to the headmaster's office.

I walked back to the village. There was nothing else I wanted to see — I was just hoping to bump into someone I knew, someone I went to school with, an old teacher, an old neighbour.

All the walking had made me thirsty, so I went into Molly's Bar. It was empty inside, although I could hear rustling from somewhere behind the bar.

After a few minutes, a young lad in a baseball cap appeared.

'A ginger ale and a packet of cheese-and-onion,' I said.

'Give me five minutes,' he replied and disappeared again.

Without waiting for him to return, I slunk out and headed back towards the church car park. I'd been up and down this same stretch of road so often that I felt ridiculous. It reminded me of that time I had a crush on a girl — oh, the tall girl with the soft brown hair — what was her name? Alison, I think — yes, it was Alison. I must have been fourteen and I'd walk or cycle up and down the road twenty times a day just hoping to see her and get a smile off her.

I collected the car and drove off north. At a petrol station in Charleville, I filled the tank and got myself a bottle of water and a chocolate bar. I went back the route I'd taken that morning as far as Athlone, and then I took some byroads around the east shore of Lough Ree. In no rush at all, I just followed the urge to drive through the heart of the country. As evening fell, the little towns looked so inviting. Couldn't I find a B&B somewhere in County Westmeath or Longford or Leitrim? I could even stay for two nights, ring in sick for work on Monday...

But a few miles past Drumshanbo, I wondered what my mother-in-law would have to say about the Lancia. She'd find some choice words, no doubt about it. Whatever else you might say about her, you never really knew what she'd come out with. She'd be camped out on the sofa, a big glass of red wine in her hand, glued to *Dancing with the Stars*. She'd be half-cut, so I'd get a really tart remark. And if I hurried home, I'd catch her before she went to bed.

*Sean Tanner*

# BLACK DOG RUNNING

It was November. As grey and dumb a month as ever there was. A dirty aul morning, the rain coming down in sheets, then drizzle. I had been sitting up all night. The black doom was on me — couldn't sleep no matter how many hot whiskeys I put away. I had that feeling, you know, that haunted feeling. The feeling that something was wrong, but you couldn't point to it because it didn't exist in the real world. It existed underneath it somewhere. A nebulous mass, faintly bulging, pulsating under the skin.

I sat in an armchair by the window, staring out to where the green ran through our park. The drizzle formed droplets on the window, and I watched them gain mass and begin to drip. I blinked out at the lone streetlight in the inky darkness and waited for the sun to come up. I had achieved an almost exquisite sense of sorrow when I spotted a lad padding by in a hi-vis — some mad yoke out running at 5 a.m on a Sunday.

Course, I remember when Carrigaline was still just a village before the pharmaceuticals moved in up the road and brought the jobs. At 5 a.m. on a Sunday morning ten, fifteen years ago, well, there wouldn't have been a sinner about the place. Not a stray fart in sight. Even the council lads took Sunday morning off. The streets abandoned to roving quarrels of grease-dappled chipper bags, forgotten fag boxes sitting lonely in the pre-dawn gloom, flights of Rizlas dancing in the wind to the tin chorus of crumpled Guinness cans clamouring down Main Street. Not even the holy rollers were up at that hour.

And do you know why? Because everyone was in bed with sick heads from the night before, like normal bloody people. They might chance getting up at ten or bribe the kids with Coco Pops and cartoons, so they could roll over and squeeze in a schnaky ride on the arse end of their drunk. Giddy with hangovers, horny with drinker's remorse and the keening surety of their own mortality. Ah yes, when death creeps in on us, we can only answer it with life. God bless the hangover ride. Sure, wasn't I a hangover baby myself.

But you had to wonder what in the name of Saint Dymphna was this fella up to at 5 a.m. on a Sunday morning? First time I saw the lad legging past, I thought he was being chased. I kept waiting for the sirens or a rabid dog to follow after in hot pursuit. But they never came. He was running for some other reason.

I was still sat there when Aileen got up. She stood in the doorway in her pyjamas, her bed hair a mad scribble of frizzy black. She put her hands on her hips when she saw me and said, 'Ah, Pat. Again?'

I ignored the question, loaded as it was, and said it to her about yer man. 'Aileen, what in God's name do you think he was at?'

'Jogging,' she said, with a yawn. 'It's all the rage these days. I've seen them at it down the Crosshaven walkway too.' Then she winced when she spotted the empty Jameson bottle at my feet.

'That bottle was half-empty already, Aileen, so don't be starting on me. But jogging? At five in the morning? Are you serious?'

'And tell us, Pat, what were you doing up at that hour? Sinking hot whiskeys and feeling sorry for yourself?'

I ignored that, knowing full well that the only way I was going to win that argument was by not having it.

'It's sick, is what it is — running on a Sunday morning? Go 'way and feck off with your running on a Sunday morning. Bunch of eejits.'

'C'mere, Pat, you'd want to get your own ducks in a row before you start throwing stones. Would you not just go and see him?'

'What for? Is Doctor Murphy going to give me my job back?'

She sighed, too tired to launch a full offensive. 'Coffee?'

'I'd murder one.'


This running... phenomenon... let's call it, seemed to have happened overnight, but it's like anything quare like that; once it catches your notice, you'll start to see it everywhere. And I tell you what, they were fecking everywhere. Rain, hail or shine, morning, noon and night. My heart went out to them, the poor craythurs, sweating and panting with tongues lolling, eyes popping, feet pounding.

It wasn't until a few weeks later, in December, that I found out what the story was for myself. By then, I really was taking the piss with the hot whiskey. It's a funny thing to find yourself at a loose end when you're not expecting it. I'd always thought it was just a job. But it was more than that. It was who you were. Now who was I? Thirty-odd years, I'd been complaining that I had no time, and then, suddenly, time was all I had.

It was another Sunday, and I'd kept Aileen up half the night with my shaky breathing and sniffing (crying, she called it). She said enough was enough. Next day she booked me in to see Doctor Murphy. I tried to fob her off as best I could.

'Ah, Aileen, 'tis just the whiskey. I'll lay off now, and I'll be grand again.'

But she was having none of it.

I was never gone on doctors myself. Fecking allergic, to be honest with you. I always thought there was something suss about them. They either knew a lot more than they pretended, or they knew a lot less. I was never sure which was worse. But sure, look it, when Aileen's on the warpath, it's always easier to just buck up and do as you're told. So off I went.

My father told me never to trust a man with smooth hands, and this fella's hands were softer than Aileen's. His handshake was watery out, too, firm enough but sort of jittery, like a stuttered sentence. You'd swear he was apologising for something. He was a slight fella with big grey caterpillar eyebrows on him that arched and wriggled as he asked after herself.

'And the toe?'

It took me a minute to realise he was referring to my last visit, which must have been some two years ago at this stage.

'Arra, grand, grand.'

'So, what can I do you for today?'

I cleared my throat, suddenly short of words. 'Well, eh. It's just I've not been sleeping, like.'

'Yeh, yeh.' His affirmations were little more than breathy whispers that put me in mind of Aileen on the phone with her sister.

'Since I was let go, like.'

'Yeh, yeh.'

'At the factory, like.'

'Yeh, yeh.'

These 'yehs' propelled me from sentence to sentence, like a stick across the arse of a stubborn donkey until, eventually, I was speaking under my own steam. I told him my head was in bits since they let me go. I told him I was fed up all the time, moping around the house like a spare prick every day, and it was driving Aileen up the walls. I left out about the whiskey. I had enough of that from herself, and I didn't need to be hearing it from him too. He listened without looking at me, his arms folded, his sloped shoulders hunched as he nodded along. His face was a practised mixture of concern and concentration.

But to be fair to the man, he wasn't a complete gowl in the end. When I finished saying my bit, he said, 'Very common.'

'Is it?'

'Very, very common these days. Especially this time of year, Merry Christmas me hole, pardon my French.'

'Sure, all I ever hear is how great everything is and how well everyone is doing.'

'Oh yes, that's the way of it, sure. The shiny happy lie of our lives must be protected at all costs. Don't ask me why. It's just the way things are. It is as though people are embarrassed about being sad these days. I don't know where people picked up the notion that life is supposed to be easy, but there it is. Nobody wants to admit it's a slog at the best of times.'

And it was true. Sure didn't I nearly just keel over from mortification telling him my own spiel.

'So it's not just me?'

'Half the country has the black doom on them.'

'Anyone I know?'

'Ah, now. They'd have me out on my ear if I told you that, but I will say this. You'd be very surprised who has it. *Very* surprised.'

And hearing that, I felt half-cured already.

'Life moves so fast these days, and we're all racing like the divil to keep up. Tinder, sure,' he said.

'Oh yes,' I said, not having a clue.

'Netflix,' he said.

'True enough, true enough.'

'Twitter.'

I nodded.

'Dabbing. Dogging. Fine Gael. Porn hub. Parking tickets. Chem sex parties. Water charges. 5G vaccines.'

There was a pause. I think he'd run out.

'Facebook?' I offered.

'Facebook,' he agreed, sadly. There was another pause while he stared blankly out the window.

'So anyway,' I leaned into him. 'What's the score, Doctor? A course of antibiotics or an injection, or what do I have to do? 'Tis only the missus says I have to get it sorted, arra, you know the way.'

He had a good long pause for himself.

'The running cure.'

'Hah?' I said, a scrap of annoyance creeping in.

'Exercise, Brendan. It's exercise. Jogging is your best bet, and anyone I prescribe it to reports back to me great success, but any kind of exercise will do.'

He went on to explain the wondrous health benefits of jogging. Neural growth pathways, reduced inflammation, and brain activity patterns that promote feelings of calm and well-being. Then he was banging on about endorphins and cortisols and all sorts of mad-sounding yokes that I hadn't a bull's notion about. It was all very official-sounding, all very professional.

'But sure, I've never done a tap of exercise in my life. I mean, I'll go for the odd walk down Myrtleville with herself, but that's about the size of it.'

'Well, now's the time to start, Brendan.' He opened his desk drawer and produced a leaflet. 'It's all in here,' he said, handing it to me.

I looked at it. There was some gommy-looking lad on the front with a huge grin and a speech bubble that came out of him saying, 'Couch to 5k in just nine weeks!'

What could I do, only shake the man's hand and thank him for his time. Fifty fucking euro for a fifteen-minute chat. I understood then what his handshake was apologising for.


I was delayed on the way home. They had a stop-go system on the main street. I stuck my head out the window for a gawk, and you'll never guess what was going on. It was the Carrigaline 5k Christmas Fun Run. They passed by on the closed lane, a whole throng of them, each sporting a Santa hat. I raised my eyes, thinking, that's more of it now. But then the penny began to drop.

I thought back to the Doctor's office. 'The running cure,' he called it. And 'Sure, half the country has the black doom on them,' he said. I looked at all those poor eejits with a new-found understanding. They were just like me. They were all depressed off their trolleys. It was a revelation. An absolute relief.

I watched them running towards me with a big smile on my face. I recalled the Doctor's words again. 'You'd be very surprised who has it.' And as I watched the heaving mass of sweaty saddos passing by, I began to recognise a few of the faces, and by God, was I surprised.

'Martin!' I exclaimed as he passed. Well, I couldn't believe it, Martin with his big house and his new car and there he was suffering the black doom just like me.

'And that's Liam, by God, Liam Cavanagh. Would you credit that?' Liam Cavanagh was the last person you'd ever suspect of being chemically imbalanced or keeping his wife up with feelings of worthlessness leaking out of his eyes at 4 a.m. on a Tuesday morning. He's the very man who'd always be smiling and telling everyone what a grand soft evening it was, but it all made sense now. He was just ashamed.

I felt a burst of compassion for the man. I rolled down the window and shouted, 'Good man, Liam, you're flying it!' He saw me in the car and gave me a thumbs-up.

As I watched them all run by, I began to feel better. I used to think I was the only miserable bollocks out there holding up the whole show with my carrying-on, but I wasn't. There are loads of us miserable bolloxes out there.

I felt a weight begin to lift. I was not alright, and that was alright. And that felt good.

And still, the runners came, hundreds of them, sweating the tears out through armpit and ass-crack before they could escape out the eyes.

They were running from their mistakes, from the past, from the future. They were straight up outrunning their sadness. But most of all, they were outrunning the notion that everything and everyone was only grand altogether. They left it behind in a cloud of dust and dirt, that shiny happy lie. And feeling lighter than I had felt in a long time, I stuck my head out the window and roared, 'Run! Run, you beautiful bastards!'

A few waved back, tongues lolling, eyes popping, feet pounding, and the black dog hot on their heels.

*Mel O'Doherty*

# TREES

He sat on the bench in the park and he watched the boys playfighting by the graveyard wall. He watched them ask passers-by for cigarettes and be refused and turn away brazen and half-mortified and the flesh of their cheeks would twitch and dimple like they were ready to cry. Two of them walked over and stood away and called out to him.

He shook his head faintly.

'Don't smoke.'

He watched them walk away. When he was their age a line of trees used to run along the back hedges of the corporation houses and stretch down the hill and out toward the bogs of Ballyphehane and he used stand at the garden end sometimes, watching them, listening. They'd sway and creak and roar; then whisper. They cheered in the gusts. Sometimes they sounded like the sea. They were silent the morning he went away, like they knew where he was going.

Even nowadays, in the grounds of the hospital, sometimes he'd hear a twig-crack in the murk under the pines and a pyjama-person would walk out, lock-armed with a relative and sometimes no one at all would come and he'd stare into them for a while like they were something malign or something lost, then bend again to his weeding. He'd go to the park and watch the children on the swings and slides and the see-saw and the babies sitting with their mothers in the grass and the men older than he who'd lost a wife and took on terriers and walked sprightly when they saw each other. And he'd watch the boys by the graveyard wall like he did now and remember the days when he was like them, before he'd stolen a bicycle, before he'd gone into Greenmount industrial school in short pants and a short-sleeved collared shirt and the shoes and socks he'd worn for his Confirmation. Before a Presentation Brother raped him his first night. Remember the days when he'd stand at the garden-end listening to the sounds of the trees.

He took the pledge for his Confirmation, the same as the other boys. Some broke it within a fortnight; stole a bottle of their father's stout or stood at the gates of Beamish & Crawford asking the men going home for a sip of the bottle in their trousers; some said they'd been there the day a barrel-top burst open when the brewery cart hit the high cobblestones at the bottom of Barrack Street; said the whole road was showered with stout; that the women had run from doorways with pots and pans and tipped a swallow into a few mouths before disappearing again. But he didn't believe them. The older boys told them the blind barman on Maylor Street was your man, if you could bluff a deep voice and the old men on stools didn't start laughing or know you from around. And that's where their Confirmation money went and a twelve-year-old temperance. The man dipped his ear to each coin and rubbed it frenziedly between thumb and forefinger, like it was a snot he was rolling, then he set it gently in the till and turned back and splayed and hopped his fingers piano-like about the counter in search of other coins. They walked out each with a pint bottle of stout stuck in their jumpers and they walked over to the north channel of the Lee and leaned over the railing and took long slugs then tucked the bottles in their clothes and talked for a while, then turned out to the river and drank again.

When they'd finished they tossed the bottles into the water and walked through Parnell Place and shouted over at girls and stepped out behind motorcars for the fumes and pushed each other and punched each other's shoulders. They walked across the south channel over to the City Hall. They walked down Anglesea Street hoping to see the Protestant nurses coming and going from the Victoria Hospital; he'd heard they kissed Catholic boys for the good it'd get them on Judgement Day. He thought of their white skirts and white stockings. The porter's bitter aftertaste scraped the glands under his earlobes when he swallowed and the pavement shifted and rose up and fell away. He might have vomited if he hadn't seen the bicycle across the road. It stood upright with the pedal set against the kerb and in the breeze the front wheel and handlebars shifted faintly like some living thing. The other boys called out to him as he crossed the road. They sounded dim and distant. Their faces were blank when he turned to them. He could hear the man shouting behind him as he cycled away.


His mother cried when the judge said the name of the place, and he cried. He and his friends used to watch the boys of St Joseph's sometimes; they'd stand on the wall across the road and go on their toes and stare into the yard until they got bored; they'd shout something into them and jump down laughing; the dirt-poor, the parentless, the bastard crimes against Jesus; criminal kids that the church rescued. The Garda called for them in the morning and they walked behind him through the streets, their low slung heads lifting now and again as if to get their bearings, like vagrants or lost tourists.

'Ma, what's a "garden ship"?' he asked.

'Don't know, boy,' she said.

'The judge said you didn't have it—or provide it—or maybe t'was I didn't—one of us anyway *lacked a garden ship.*'

'Oh... guardianship!'

'Ya, ya. That was it. Guardianship.'

'Fucker! A lot he'd know about it. A woman cleaning the church for a few shillings and a dead husband and a growing child and nothing coming in. An' he looking down at me! D'ya think he's familiar with the steps of the Vincent de Paul's?'

She fussed at the collar of her coat.

'I'm sorry, Ma,' he said.

She took her hand from her collar and slid a knuckle down his cheek and looked at him then turned out again to the road and narrowed her eyes as if answers and explanations were out there, memories shooting across the mind's horizon.

They walked through the big gates of St Joseph's Industrial School and went across the yard; things were scraped in the stone that he read as he passed over them, fresh white scrawlings and older ones and dull gougings with no colour at all. The Garda knocked at the big green doors and they came up behind him and stood there waiting in the silence. A Brother opened the door and looked down at them and nodded grimly. The Garda caught him by the elbow and walked him through the doors. The Brother stepped out of the way and spoke to his mother.

''Twill be Christmas Day you can visit,' he said. 'He'll be grand till then.'

She'd already begun to walk away.

'A new boy, you'll be thinking,' he said.

He watched his mother walk across the yard toward the big gate; the wind blew and she held the neck of her coat to keep it fastened and her handbag hung low and spun faintly and her heels scraped on the stone like a low cadent moaning.

The Brother walked up a long hallway, tiled in red and black, and the boy followed behind watching the black robes shift and sway and he thought of the crows in the schoolyard after the bell went. By the windows, the white painted walls were bubbled and flaking. They went up to the dormitory and walked down the centre of the room and the boy glanced at the length of beds either side and thought of the cars queuing on St Patrick's Street. The Brother stopped and pointed at a bed. A grey wool jumper and short trousers lay upon it and a beige shirt hung by the collar from the bedpost. The Brother turned away and did not speak while the boy undressed and put on the clothes. They walked up the dormitory again. There was a statue of Jesus over the doorway. His arms were cast out and open, as if he were weighing something.

They walked down the stairs and down a long hallway. He could hear the workshop hammerings from way off; their steps fell in and out with it. He was shown into the room and the religious nodded at each other and the door closed behind him. The boys watched him from under their eyebrows then went on with their cabinets, running their palms over the tops then sliding thumb and finger down the frames, bending to drawer boxes and glides, running knuckles along inner-shelves, rendering a tool upon a hinge or handle. After some time, the Brother came to him, looked into his face and said nothing. He walked away, beckoning him over his shoulder. Halfway up the room he stopped and pointed to a group of boys.

'Watch,' the brother said and continued on up the room.

He stood and watched them work. They sawed and cut and hammered and their eyes trailed down their cabinets and out toward his shoes and withdrew again and he watched the wood chippings on the table and the sawdusted hair of the boys' arms and he thought of the trees over the back garden that morning. They'd been quiet and the new light sparkled in the spaces between the leaves.

He woke in the dark and a Brother was sitting on his bed just watching him with the light of the moon on his face and on his collar. He could hear the woken breaths of other boys and the low squeals of their beds as if tiny tortures were playing out in the dark. He rose and followed the Brother and the low whispers fell in behind him; he could see the light of the doorway up ahead and the outstretched arms of Jesus and the stone creases of his robes and he watched Him all the way into the light.

He bled in the night and in the morning another child placed a tub of Sudocreme beside him as they lay huddled. He opened it. It looked like the icing on his mother's Christmas cake. He stared up at the boy, wondering.

''Twill help,' the other said.

The boy's hair was thin and limp and the scabs of nail-scrawls criss-crossed his scalp and his eyes were dull and shineless like the low-tide puddles on the mudflats of the river. His lips trembled as he spoke as if weakened by it or new to it. He'd see many like him in the three years that followed: orphans sent up from the Sisters of Mercy or the Good Shepherds or Rushbrooke in Cobh, institutional children who'd never known a mother and father, who'd come of age at eleven or twelve and passed from the nuns to the Brothers, passed along the cataclysmic trinity of mother and baby home to orphanage to industrial school. 'Noughts' they were called, for that's what they had in this world and all they'd ever have.

When he got out of St Joseph's a Garda found him a cleaning job in the TB sanitorium that Noel Browne had set up out in Glanmire. When his mother died the corporation took her house back and so the hospital gave him a tiny room off the cellar where the clean spare mattresses and the pine disinfectant of his labours were kept and he was happy there for Dr Browne had insulated the place well and kept it warm and spotless and he had played his part and he was proud of that, his own little daily killing of TB. And when the disease was gone, the sanitorium became a mental hospital for the clear-outs from Our Lady's and St Kevin's on the Lee Road, and he became the groundsman. He was still there; fifteen years a sanitorium cleaner and thirty-three years a mental hospital groundsman.

He shook his head and spat between his legs. He looked across to the boys by the wall. They hunched and huddled over a cigarette, like it was some beloved thing, prodigal and tenuous. Some of the boys leant against the wall and some sat on the ground and the Celtic crosses of priests' graves grouped behind their heads like the congress of some other order and way off the stained glass circle on the church gable seemed like a black sun or the petals of some perilous flower. He sat back and stretched his arms along the back rest and he stared for a long time at the sky, listening to the children playing in the park and their mothers calling them and the boys away by the wall and the garrulous Protestant nurses from the Victoria Hospital a long time ago and the noughts who'd come in his nightmares and sit about him for days.

He felt a drizzle, and then a gentle rain. He rose off the bench and walked along the path toward the road and he walked along the road for the mile and a half it took. The rain fell away for a while, then came back again; he was glad to see the big white gates of the hospital. He passed through the gates and started up the avenue, looking in the grass as he went. There were trees there once, clustered birches put down in Dr Browne's time and behind them a few alders and white ashes and every autumn their leaves littered the lawns and avenue and choked the drains until one day he got the order to cut them down. So he did, he cut them down in the prime of their youths. He spent weeks digging out the stumps with a spade and pick-axe and pulling up the muddy roots with his bare hands.

Now he stepped off the tarmacadam and turned and walked in the grass down toward the road again and he could feel the earth dip and dimple where the trees had been and when he got to the gates he turned and came back over the grass and then he turned again and he did this over and over. After a while he stopped and lowered himself down and pulled up his knees to his chest and locked them with his arms and he stayed like that for a long, long time, picturing the trees he'd cut down and talking to them, and in the evening a nurse came down the avenue and helped him up from the grass and he stretched and brushed his clothes with his hands and for a while he just stood and watched the grass flick and twitch where he'd sat, then they walked together out of the gentle rain.

*Tina Pisco*

# DECLAN'S SISTER

When Declan asked me to come around for his sister's eighteenth I was well up for it, but the minute I walked in I knew this was going to be the worst house party ever. All the lights were on, even the neon strip lighting in the kitchen. There were two lads in the corner surfing porn on a laptop. Another five lads were crowded around the telly playing Metal Gear Solid on a PS2. Actually, only one of them was playing. The other four were just sitting there watching. A shiny 'Happy eighteenth!' banner was strung limply over the curtain rail. A few bags of Taytos were strewn across the coffee table. No one had even bothered to put any music on.

Declan works at the Texaco on the outskirts of town. We'd been friends back in primary school, but we drifted apart in secondary school. We don't really see much of each other since I went away to college. I'd passed all my exams and was down for the summer. I was thinking of just chucking it all in, even though I only had one more year to go. I wasn't sure if I could stick another lonely year up in Dublin.

'You free Friday?' he asked as he handed me back my change. 'It's my little sister's eighteenth. At my gaff. If you're not doing anything, like?'

It sounded like a great idea. I couldn't remember his sister's name. I figured someone would mention it at the party.

The house was on one of those estates that had mushroomed like fairy rings around every West Cork town thanks to the Celtic Tiger boom; a pokey little house on the end of a row of identical tiny, pokey little houses. I had come with a bottle of Captain Morgan's, a bag of weed and enough Red Bull to sink a submarine. I sat down on the sofa and started skinning up.

'You can't smoke,' said Angela as she waddled down the stairs. 'The baby is asleep.'

I wanted to ask if it would be OK when the baby was awake but thought better of it and just brushed the weed back in the bag. Declan had recently become a dad after a one-night stand with Angela. I feel sorry for the poor fecker. One drunken shag, and a year later, here he was in a tiny little house with a giant mammy for a girlfriend and a kid asleep upstairs. I smiled my sexiest smile for Angela. She didn't smile back. I grabbed my gear and fled into the garden.

I was amusing myself by blowing smoke rings when I heard the creak of a swing I hadn't noticed in the darkness. I thought it was a child until she stepped into the light.

'Hi, Rob,' she said. 'I bet you don't remember me.'

She was small, skinny and as flat as a pancake everywhere

except for her nose. Her nose was long, thin and sharp enough to cut a line with. She smelt strongly of chips. She stood shivering, in a bright pink nylon dress that hung on her like washing on a line. Her ankles were fake-tan blotchy and looked about to break as she teetered on a pair of gold stiletto sandals. A large badge was pinned to her dress. It read: Eighteen Today!

'I sold you a breast in a bun and onion rings last Christmas,' she said leaning back against the wall. 'I work in the chipper. Full time, like. I've got the night off seeing as it's my birthday. You didn't recognise me, but I knew it was you.'

I passed her the bottle to cover my discomfort. I still couldn't remember her name.

'Happy Birthday!' I sang. 'Declan's sister — all grown up! I can't believe you're eighteen!' I took a long drag and blew a perfect smoke ring. It lingered over her head like a halo. 'Look! You're an angel.'

She took a giant gulp of rum and blushed a deep pink that was a perfect match for her dress. I should have noticed the crazy in her eyes. I should have walked straight out of there and found another place to get wasted on that fine Friday night in smalltown West Cork. I should have, but I didn't. I stayed with Declan's sister, passing the bottle back and forth, smoking the joint, spouting more and more rubbish as she looked on in awe, rolling another, smoking that one too until we'd finished the bottle and I couldn't roll anymore without the help of a flat surface. The last thing I remember is dancing with her as we belted out 'Buffalo Soldier'.

I got the first text as I slept off my drunk. I muted my phone and went back to sleep. When I woke up there were three messages from Declan's sister. She'd signed the first one **Smoke Angel**. I sent back a smiley face. She sent back a heart. I turned off my phone.

I went sailing with friends down around Glandore for the weekend. I kept my phone off. I told myself that the reception was crap, but really, I was avoiding Declan's sister. I still didn't know her name. When I got home and turned my phone back on, there were fifteen messages and four voicemails from her. I deleted them all without opening them.

I was strolling down Main Street deep in thought when I walked straight into her. I didn't recognise her at first. Her hair was scraped back flat against her head, and she wore a grey tracksuit and a white smock like the tea ladies at school used to wear.

'There you are!' she yelped. 'Why didn't you answer your phone?'

I started to tell her about the bad reception, but she wasn't listening. She lifted herself up on her tippy toes and brought her mouth as close to my ear as she could manage.

'I can't stay. I had to cover for Francine again because she has the vomiting bug. She's probably grand — the bitch. Probably has a hangover. No one's minding the chipper. I ran out when I saw you. I'll lose my job if he finds out.'

Then she took a small jump and pecked my mouth before sauntering off. I felt like I'd been nipped by a terrier. I wanted to call her back and explain that there had been some mistake, but I still couldn't remember her name. I must have looked distraught because Mrs Murphy, the school secretary, stopped and gave me a little pity tap on the shoulder. She was all misty-eyed and smiling.

'Ah to be young again and in love,' she sighed. 'Don't worry. She'll be back.'

By the time I got back to my car, five people had asked me where I'd been last weekend. It seems that Declan's sister had been working double shifts and had asked every single person who'd been to the chipper if they knew where I was. They all seemed to think that something was going on between us, but not one of them could tell me her name.

I got the first text at around midnight. I was minding the house while my parents went on a mid-week hotel break in Killarney.

Hey! Bufulo Soldier!

A few hours of smoke and a half a bottle of Jack Daniel's that Dad wouldn't miss had left me nice and mellow. I texted back:

Watsup?

I figured there was no reason to ignore the poor girl. There was no harm in being friendly. It would be my good deed for the day. I rolled myself another one for being a kind and caring human being as I considered a short and witty reply. I was sparking up when my phone delivered another text.

U no the x boyfriend I told u about?

I didn't remember. I giggled to myself.

Which one?

This was going well. How bad could it be anyway? It was just a few text messages to cheer up what's-her-face. I was trying to devise a cool way to get her to reveal her name without having to ask when she replied.

LOL!!! The only boyfriend before you, silly!! The one who was in prison!

Before *you*? In *prison*? *Was* in prison? I was still trying to decipher that when she texted again.

They let him out. He's outside revving the motor. My Dad's going mental.

Her parents lived on one of the older estates in the middle of town. I pictured a big, burly ex-con-boyfriend with his foot flat on the accelerator, while Declan's dad sat in the front room foaming at the mouth, banging a Chinese gong. I decided to wait and see. I threw on *Face Off* as a comforting distraction and switched my phone to silent.


This is where it gets crazy. Right at my favourite part of the film (when Nicolas Cage is having sex with John Travolta's wife—except it's really John Travolta pretending to be Nicolas Cage pretending to be him), I noticed I'd missed a text.

He knows about us. He kidnapped me!!!

I stared at the phone in my hand. I closed my eyes and tried willing it to self-destruct. I jumped when it started to vibrate.

He's got me in a bungalow on the beach. Next to the caravan park.

I fumbled as I hit reply.

Call the Guards

No credit! ☺

The smiley face reassured me. I muted the film but kept on watching. I was feeling a bit groggy. I waited another few minutes and then decided that everything would probably be fine if I went to sleep. I was just nodding off when the phone started vibrating again. On the screen Travolta as Nicolas Cage held a gun to his daughter's head while Nicolas Cage, as Travolta, looked on in horror. It's a tense moment. I nearly shat myself when the phone danced across the coffee table and fell on the floor.

Come and save me!

What about boyfriend?

He's asleep. Be my hero!

I could feel a whole lot of stupid coming on. I blame it on
Nicolas Cage. Or maybe it was John Travolta. I grabbed my
mother's car keys and headed out the door.

A big yellow moon hung over the ocean spotlighting four
identical holiday homes. Sand had swept up over the road and
sparkled in the moonlight. The first three bungalows were
dark, but the last one had a small light on over the door and a
black BMW parked in the drive. I crept up as quietly as I could
and listened.

I could do this. It was a piece of piss. This final act of lunacy
would sort everything out. All I had to do was slip in the back,
find Declan's sister and get her back to town. I'd take her up to
the Garda station to make a complaint. Then she'd *have* to tell
them her name. Bingo. Best of all, when the guard asked if she
was my girlfriend, I'd say, 'No, Garda. I'm just a friend helping
my mate's sister.' Brilliant. Problem solved. It was genius, really.

I scuttled across the yard and crept around the house.
A light was shining through an open sliding door; a curtain
flapped gently, casting shadows onto the patio. I slid over the
sand, parted the curtain — and froze.

A hairy, writhing mass of a man was sprawled on the
carpet, grinding away at the woman under him. It looked to me
as if Declan's sister and her con ex-boyfriend were on the way to
reconciliation. I decided to leave them at it. Sprinting for my car,
I slipped on the sand and twisted my ankle, yelping as I reeled
around like a proper Looney Tune, which sounds funny except

that it hurt like hell. I heard a loud grunt from the house and a gruff male voice bellowed:

'Who's there? Who the fuck is that?'

He may have been fat and hairy, but he was fast. Before I could take off, he tackled me to the ground. I lay flat on my face, sand in my nose and mouth, as he pinned me down. It felt like a whale had landed on my back.

'Don't worry Sheila! I've got him!' the man yelled. 'I've got everything under control.'

The smell of sweat and sex enveloped me, but all I could think was 'Sheila! Her name is Sheila!' He pulled me up and gave me a few slaps. I closed my eyes to avoid seeing his furry, naked belly and waggling half-erect penis.

Sheila was screaming. 'Stop! Stop, it Mick!' Except that it didn't sound like Declan's sister. The voice was definitely older. 'Stop slapping him, Mick. Can't you see! It's Robert. John and Mary's boy.'

I cocked one eye open. Standing before me, like a gorilla in the moonlight, was my Uncle Mick. Framed in the doorway, a curtain draped around her naked body was Mrs Murphy.

'Get back inside, Sheila,' said Uncle Mick, pulling me up to my feet and brushing me off. Mrs Murphy vanished in a white flash of flesh. Then, summoning a level of dignity that I will admire until my dying day, Uncle Mick held me by both shoulders, looked me straight in the eye and said, 'We will never speak of this again.'

That suited me just fine.

As I sat back in the car, I noticed my phone flashing.

Holding Out for a Hero is my favourite Song. No other boyfriend. Only YOU!!! What's your favourite song?

When my parents got home the next morning I had already packed. Dennis was driving up and would give me a lift. I told my mother that I had to go back to Dublin right away. I mumbled something about getting an early start at my last year in college. She raised an eyebrow and looked at me.

'What about Declan's sister?' she asked.

'What about her?' I replied.

'Mary McCarthy told Kathleen that you two were doing a line,' Mum said. 'I told Kathleen that seemed unlikely, but you never know.' She stepped back and took a good look at me. 'So, nothing going on there?'

'Nope,' I said beaming my best mum-pleasing smile. 'Never was.'

'Good. I'm glad,' Mum lowered her voice. 'She's far from the best-looking one in her family and that's saying something. Poor craytur has her father's nose. Not the sharpest knife in the drawer either.' Mum paused to rearrange some white lilies in the hall. I picked up my bags and headed for the door. 'What's her name again?' she asked as she kissed me goodbye.

'Whose name?'

'Declan's sister?'

'I haven't a clue,' I answered, giving her a big hug before darting out of the house and into the car that would take me back to the sanity of the capital.

I threw the SIM card out the window somewhere on the Curragh in Kildare. I figured that was far away enough to be safe.

*Mary Morrissy*

# LOST PROPERTY

Carmel Dromey stands with a knot of people at the gates of Lichfield Cottage in Ballintemple. Through the bars she can see the long low house with its church-shaped dormer windows and gingerbready eaves, which the *Examiner* called the Strawberry Hill gothic style. Carmel is a hungry reader of property supplements and she has always lusted after this house. Now it could be hers! The viewing is set for 11:00, but there is no sign of the auctioneer. He arrives ten minutes late, just as the group has begun getting restive, tired of smiling at one another reassuringly as if they were queue comrades at a bus stop.

'Apologies, folks,' Richie Barker (according to his lanyard) says breezily as he walks among them with a sheaf of brochures under his armpit. He's electively bald but with a blue five o'clock shadow where the regrowth is starting so he's like a baby-man. He's dressed in a tight navy suit and a white shirt. But his skewed tie and trainers give off a dress-down Friday vibe. He pushes open the elaborate double gates of Lichfield and ushers the group of six, including Carmel, into the gravelled driveway. Behind him, Carmel gets the impression of a tended leafy garden.

'Well, folks,' Richie says folksily, 'as you know we have a charming historic property here. Once home of George Boole, world-famous mathematician and father of computer science. Founder of Boolean mathematics.' Richie pauses. 'You know, the and/or option you use for internet searches?'

Carmel does know. She has measured out her middle age in night classes. Her most recent foray into Adult Ed has been 'Historic Corkonians'. (When she saw the course advertised, she'd read it as Cork Onions. *Know your Cork Onions*, they should call it, she'd thought.) George Boole was on the syllabus. It's the first class she's taken since being made a widow. She likes the designation — makes her sound statuesque.

It's three years since she lost Ray. Ray, once beloved, who plunged the family into bankruptcy in 2017 when his chain of betting shops went belly-up. He'd had to go off to England for a year leaving Carmel on her own to face the music. He'd forced the sale of her beloved house and sunk the proceeds into a penthouse apartment in the Elysian Tower in Carmel's name. She'd lived there in solitary splendour while he weathered his year of financial exile in a bed-sit in Reading. And she's still stuck up there five years later.

'How bad,' her friend Jacinta had said to her. 'I wouldn't mind being given a fancy apartment for my very own.'

But Carmel didn't see the penthouse as having anything to do with her. It was just where Ray had installed her, a vessel for hiding money. Nothing was right about the place. She realised that when her daughter Louise came to visit with the twins. There was too much slip and slide on the glacially-tiled floors, too many sharp corners on the designer furniture. The coffee table had knife-edges, the steel-cold kitchen was full of traps such as the toothed waste disposal unit. The occluded handles of the cabinets seemed designed to enrage the kids, suggesting entry, then denying it. There was no safe outdoor space, bar the Japanese garden at ground level; the balcony was a no-go area. Harry was happy to watch *PAW Patrol* on his iPad but the floor-to-ceiling plate-glass windows in the cavernous living room distressed Megan, who was one of those kids who wouldn't look you in the eye. She'd howled and howled the first time she'd seen the vertiginous view. Even with the curtains drawn, the child was mesmerically drawn to the awful drop, pushing back the heavy brocade drapes and the flame-coloured muslin nets behind them, to peer down at the ground far below. This would set off a fresh round of torment that couldn't be assuaged. Louise would have to carry her off, a furious ball of rage. Carmel could hear her shrieks echoing down the elevator shaft, all sixteen floors of it, and found it chimed with a desolate protest of her own. She couldn't be a granny in this place and as time went on, she wondered if she'd ever wanted to be a granny at all. Unsurprisingly, Louise's visits soon petered out.

Ray Junior did his visiting duties standing up. He paced up and down as if he was waiting to be brought into a boardroom to be fired. Carmel could feel his disapproval of her new surroundings. She wanted to say this isn't my choice either. Afterwards, he would trek down to the underground garage at the Elysian and start Ray's Audi, another useless thing in her name.

Carmel had never learned to drive. It terrified her. Her father had been a forklift driver. Once when her mother was ill, he'd taken her to work with him. He'd done tricks with the forks, spearing a tower of empty pallets and raising them up and down on the mast. Then he put her sitting in the cab. Through the windscreen she could see the prongs protruding like a pair of medieval battering rams. Every time she imagined driving, that was what she saw.

After Louise was born, Ray had urged her to take lessons.

'I'll buy you a little run-around,' he'd said.

Her school pal Dee said she'd take her on practice runs in the Tesco car park after hours.

'Look, girl, if I can drive, any fecking eejit can.'

But Carmel baulked. She couldn't justify her fear of driving to herself, so how could she to anyone else? She used the money Ray had dished out for the driving lessons to hire Margaret Bird. Margaret was supposed to be a cleaner, but she did school runs and packed lunches and everything in between. Even with the kids long gone, Margaret still came. If anything, she mothered Carmel with her constant round of advice. If you asked Carmel, Margaret had been a much better investment than any car, until she, too, had to be liquidated on Ray's instruction.

'You know what that car really needs,' Ray Junior would mutter darkly when he emerged from underground to throw the car keys in a glass bowl on the kitchen island with the clatter of gunfire.

'What?' Carmel had asked.

'The fuck driven out of it,' he said.

But Ray Junior wouldn't oblige. He refused to drive it on principle. If he didn't approve of Carmel's new accommodations, he was contemptuously ashamed of his father.

Only Amy, in France, was intrigued by Carmel's new situation. All she wanted was for Carmel to steer her through the penthouse on the laptop so that she could take it all in. (Ray had bought the flat complete with fixtures and furnishings so everything was to someone else's taste.)

Carmel couldn't stop comparing the penthouse with Carmond, the wreck of a house Ray had bought shortly after they were married. It was he who had come came up with the name. Where Carmel came from, houses didn't have names.

'Carmel loves Raymond,' he'd said when he staggered over the threshold carrying her, four months pregnant with Louise, 'and together we make "Carmond".'

But it was Carmel who had made it a warm, welcoming home. Fraying at the edges perhaps, bald patches on the rugs and the elbows of arm chairs, but cherished from tender use. The house's scuffs and scars were emotional; it was honest wear-and-tear. Carmel had felt bonded to that house in a way she couldn't explain, not even to Ray. It was something she had created single-handed out of a semi-tenement reeking of dry rot and mouldy with rising damp. (It was the sort of place her 'great-greats' might have been crowded into paying rents to rack landlords.)

Ray, having named it, had lived in Carmond carelessly; he had a rat-run of favoured sites — the armchair in front of the television, the kitchen counter where he often wolfed down meals on the run, his side of the bed where racing newspapers, betting stubs and windowed envelopes washed up in a tide on the carpet. But otherwise, he barely left a footprint. He had no opinions on furniture or décor; she could have painted the whole place in shocking pink and he wouldn't have noticed. In the end, his indifference showed. He'd treated Carmond as an asset that could be stripped, making Carmel feel like an over-the-hill pole-dancer. In one fell swoop he had dismantled the meaning of their life together.

'I'm doing this for all of us,' he'd said pleadingly as he cleared a patch in the middle of her dahlias in the front garden for the auctioneer's placard. For full visibility, he'd said. For a quick sale is what he meant.

That night, the wrought iron front gate was stolen from the house. An opportunistic theft, Ray said, they saw the sign. It upset Carmel that her beloved house had been flogged off looking like a child missing its front tooth.


Richie leads them into the hallway where he sets down a clipboard on a delicate-legged, half-moon table and asks them to sign in. To frighten off the rubber-neckers, Carmel suspects, those only here for a good snoop. Not like her.

'The Booles moved to Lichfield because it was close to Blackrock train station, and Professor Boole could take the train directly to college,' Richie is saying. 'The station is long gone but the prospective owner will have access to the lovely Leeside greenway, a terrific amenity.'

'I suppose you know,' Carmel says as she stoops to sign her name, 'that Boole's wife was very clever too. She was a self-taught mathematician.'

'Is that so,' Richie says. He swirls the clipboard around and stares at her name. 'Dromey, are you anything to do with the betting shop crowd?'

There was no escape from it. For the year Ray was away, Carmel had kept her sights low and her head down. When she went out, she felt she should wear a black, fine mesh veil with tiny rosettes on it like a Mafia widow, though at that stage it was Carmond she was in mourning for, not Ray. She passed people on the streets whom she knew Ray had put out of work. She recognised some of the faces from the Christmas free bar Ray used to host at the Ambassador every year. She also knew they recognised her but they didn't shout at her or shake their fists. In fact, it was she who felt tempted to shout at them— *It wasn't me!*

Her friends and Carmond neighbours had drifted away. Dee blamed her breast cancer, Jacinta the cost of parking in the city centre. It was as if living in the tower had removed Carmel to another realm, and it was true, in a way; she'd become a high-rise resident of Nowheresville. Jacinta kept on saying, come on over to our place. But Carmel couldn't bear to go back to St Luke's and not be going home to Carmond. She couldn't pass it by and know it had been farmed out to someone else. It's only bricks and mortar, that's what Ray kept on saying; how he'd changed his tune! But for her, Carmond was like a fourth child in their marriage whom Ray had sold into slavery.

Carmel thought it best to give up the night classes while Ray was away. She'd just finished 'The Victorian Poets' and was signed up for 'French Impressionism' and 'Ancient Greece: Myths and Legends'. Alone in the tower and without the crutch of further education, she'd had plenty of time to wonder how things had got to this pass. Had she missed something in the run-up to the collapse of the Dromey empire? Had Ray sent up flares about his financial distress? But no, that wasn't his style. He'd never been one to bring work home. Let me take care of the money, he used to say. So she let him. He was the breadwinner. When she wanted something, he'd unfold a wad of cash and hand it over. She was a home-maker, that was her end of the bargain.

Because Ray had inherited the business, Carmel had always presumed it came naturally to him until she saw the hunted look in his eye that night when he declared Carmond would have to go.

'I've had sleepless nights over this,' he'd said, reaching out and squeezing her hand as they sat in the sitting room with the TV sound turned off. 'I'm a wreck.'

When he said it, she saw the bruised shadows under his eyes but up until then she hadn't noticed anything amiss.

It wasn't that they'd grown apart. Ray had expended all his romantic energy in the early years on winning her, and having won her, providing for her. He showed his love in his financial constancy, not with displays of affection. So when she'd come in from a class agog with her latest discoveries — the mysteries of Pompei, the splendours of Rome — he'd look up from his recliner and say, 'It's alright, Carm, I don't need a blow-by-blow.' It wasn't cruelty; it was a kind of heedlessness. Despite all their years together, he'd never properly understood that the night courses were her badges of honour, although for a girl from the Buildings, no amount of extra-mural classes could make up for the low horizons she'd started with.

She and Ray had been together since her teens. She'd quit school at fifteen to look after her father and brothers after her mother died. But as the boys got older, she'd got a part-time job during school hours on the till at Dromey's. The money came in handy given her father's precarious employment, particularly after the accident. But it wasn't just that. She didn't want to become a maiden aunt, the kind of woman who grew old and whiskery, playing mother to children who weren't her own and tending an ageing father who'd turn her into a spinster.

'Your poor mother was a saint,' her father used to lament.

And I won't be a martyr, Carmel thought silently.

Ray had interviewed her for the job. Within a year she was going out with him. He'd made all the running. He'd pacified his own father who thought anyone from the Buildings must be a slapper or a gold-digger. He'd seen off her father's resistance to a Pres boy sniffing around her by insisting on paying for the wedding reception at the Imperial. He'd arranged everything; well, he *was* the boss's son. Carmel had distrusted Ray's certainty about her, about them. But she'd abdicated to it, happy to be swept up in an upward movement out of the Buildings. No one had ever fought for her before. That must mean something, she'd thought.

The longer she lived alone in the Elysian, the more Carmel suspected that her marriage might not survive the break. But after his year of purdah, Ray came back and where else was he going to go? There were two of them now rattling around in the glass palace. Ray no longer had work to go to, so he was under her feet all day. It annoyed her that Ray kept on admiring all the things she found disorienting about the penthouse — the lofty, disabling views, the merciless appurtenances. Oh this is nifty, he would say, tricking with the built-in coffee maker, or trying out the waste disposal unit. He delighted in swinging from the hanging rattan chair which had had to be unhooked from a beam in the ceiling every time the children came. A basket case, she thought sourly. If he felt bad about putting one hundred and sixty people out of work, it didn't show. He seemed unscathed by the experience. He adapted to the lifestyle of an unemployed man with the same appetite that he had run the business. He rose late and watched television in the afternoon with the drapes drawn. Sports channels, of course, his former occupation now a full-time hobby. Horse-racing, European football, mixed martial arts. It was like the Coliseum in the echoey living room, the air filled with the sounds of male gladiatorial combat.

She'd thought that once Ray was back, normal service would resume.

'Can we get it back?' she asked him.

'Get what back?'

'Carmond.'

'Have you understood nothing?' he said.

'It was the only place I felt myself.' She knew she sounded whiney but it was true.

'Oh please,' Ray said. 'Look around you. Most people would kill for this.'

It was then she directed him towards the second bedroom. She would never pardon him for allowing her to live in a fool's paradise.

Lockdown had been a blessing at first. Suddenly everyone was living like her and Ray — under siege. Masked and gloved, she went to Aldi in the basement once a week to do the shop. Ray had taken up running in Reading. He did a loop around Centre Park Road under cover of dark. Sheathed in black Lycra, he looked like a portly cat burglar. They spoke to the kids over Zoom. Louise lined the twins up in front of the screen and made them wave. Even Megan accidentally caught Carmel's eye once or twice and didn't flinch. Amy had started giving Carmel French lessons online in preparation for the time when she and Ray would be able to visit. They seemed to be approaching a kind of normality, or as normal as things could be living in an eyrie in a time of plague with a broken husband who'd failed her.

But then Ray upped and died.

Well, no, there was nothing up about it because he'd been downed by Covid, like an aircraft shot out of the sky. In all her years nursing her kids, Carmel had never seen anything like it. It was like watching someone drown in clogged mud. She could see his outstretched hands waving like a swimmer in difficulties but she could do nothing to help. The ambulance men who came to take him away were shrouded in plastic head to toe with masks, shower caps on their heads, pampooties on their feet like police pathologists from a TV show visiting a crime scene.

'Don't leave me,' Ray had said to her as the doors of the ambulance were slammed shut.

Was this his punishment? Carmel wondered.

She succumbed to a stifling passivity after Ray was taken away. She didn't, couldn't fight for him. She blamed the Covid restrictions which meant she couldn't visit him in hospital and when she phoned the ward, no one answered. Now she wondered was it her bridling rage about Carmond that had stopped her championing Ray's case? Or had she simply 'let' him die? Three days after he was admitted, she had to say goodbye on the mobile phone before he was intubated. She looked into his eyes and saw an alien terror behind his mask. She had to do all the talking because he couldn't. She told him she loved him. What else was she going to say with a nurse in blue gloves holding the phone at his end eavesdropping on every word?

It wasn't a lie. She had loved him, but it just wasn't in her to forgive him. Even after he was gone. There was an impoverished funeral in an empty church with just the family. Amy watched remotely. Carmel knew Ray had bought a grave plot but she didn't want to have a permanent monument to him. Wasn't she living in that? She opted for cremation. When the urn came, she tipped the ashes into the waste disposal unit.

The visitors scatter through the house once Richie has finished his spiel. Carmel is in the main bedroom alone when he catches up with her, luxuriating in the summery light which bathes the entire house in a benign graciousness. She has successfully imagined herself into Lichfield. Into the lovely living room with the French windows, the Persian runner and the grand piano, the rustic kitchen with the Aga and the country pine table, or being abed here in the mornings, adrift on the soft white bed linen and the bowing branches of wisteria crowding at the window. She sees her reflection in the gold-framed mirror over the mantelpiece and she doesn't look out of place. Then a thought strikes her.

'I wonder if this is the room he died in?' she says to Richie. He looks at her askance.

'Boole, I mean.'

'Oh,' Richie says and tries to jolly his way out of it. 'I'm afraid that's not the kind of info we have on our specs.'

'You know there were those who said Mrs Boole was responsible for her husband's demise.'

'You don't say,' Richie says.

'The professor had got soaked in a downpour after walking to the campus. He delivered a full day's lectures in wet clothes. When he came down with a cough and a cold, Mrs Boole called in a doctor who was a believer in hydrotherapy who suggested he be wrapped in wet bed sheets as a cure, on the principle of treating the illness with the cause.'

'Poor sod!' Richie says.

'Oh come on,' she appeals to him. 'He was a brilliant mathematician studying logic. Why did nobody ever question *his* logic? Teaching in damp robes all day. Sure any fool knows that's asking for trouble.'

'Maybe his wife secretly wanted rid of him,' Richie says.

He's been streaming too many true crime serials, Carmel thinks.

'Oh no,' she says. 'It was a very happy marriage — they had five children.'

'So did my olds but that proves nothing,' Richie says glumly. For a moment she sees him not as a shiny-headed young Turk, but as an overlooked child of warring parents, and she feels a stab of pity for him.

'So,' he says, and there's an odd hostile glint in his eye. 'You're *not* related to that Dromey guy then?'

The truce is over.

She takes a deep breath.

'Yes, I am,' she says evenly. 'But that chapter is closed.'

'For some, maybe,' Richie says. 'My father worked for Dromey's all his life and they threw him out on the street with nothing.' There was a little crack in his voice.

'It broke him,' Richie says. 'Broke him and killed him.'

An image of her own father flashes into Carmel's head. A weak man giving off drink fumes who'd killed a workmate by impaling him with the blades of the forklift. It was an accident, he kept on saying, but Carmel remembered the tricks he'd done for her in the warehouse, like a pilot doing loop-the-loops at an air spectacular.

'I mean, literally killed him,' Richie insists.

Dead air seems to reverberate around the words as if he'd shouted them. 'I'm sorry.' It's out before Carmel can stop it.

She looks around to see if anyone else has heard. But she and Richie are alone, stranded in the odd intimacy of strangers in an unfamiliar bedroom.

'I'm sorry,' she repeats while inside her head the old chorus gets louder — *It's not my fault.* 'My husband,' she begins but it's as if Richie has heard her inner voice.

'Nothing to do with you, that's what you're going to tell me, I suppose,' Richie says. 'You're just the wife.'

The widow, she wants to say, but then she thinks of Ray's lonely death. She thinks of his ashes travelling in clouds down the waste chute and the lie she told the children that the funeral home had lost them. She feels a huge sob well up in her throat. She tries to swallow it back down. She can't be the one weeping; she knows that much. She rummages in her bag for a tissue.

'I'm sorry,' she says for the third time.

Richie changes tack.

'And where would you be moving from, Mrs Dromey?'

'I'm in the Elysian,' she says, relieved at the change of mood. 'For the moment.'

'I see,' Richie says in a light testy way. 'It's well for some.'

'Look,' she begins but one of the other viewers comes into the room and asks: 'Is there an en suite?'

Richie gathers himself and puts on his work expression.

'Let me show you, Sir.'

Carmel is left alone. A shower is turned on in the en suite and she can hear Richie crooning about the plumbing. A sweat of shadow peels over the room as the sun goes behind cloud outside. Goose pimples rise on her arms. It's as if the dead have gathered in the room — Boole, her father, Richie's father. And Ray. Always Ray. She feels oddly spent. Her apology has dissipated the rage of years. Now what? She crushes the auctioneer's bumpf in her hand, feeling her own monstrosity in these genteel surroundings. But she lingers in Lichfield all the same, clinging to the last remnants of her property libido. She's the last to leave, Richie clicking the bolts shut on the gates behind her. There'll be no moving on for her. She thinks of 'The Lady of Shalott' from her poetry course. *The mirror crack'd.* That's her. She'll end her days as a prisoner in the tower. That'll be her reparation.

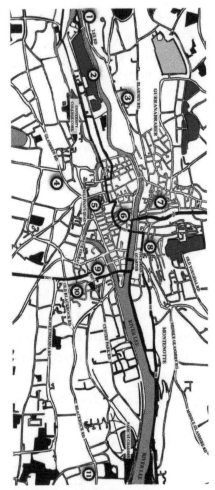

## Story Location Map of Cork City

1. *Trees* by Mel O'Doherty: Lee Road
2. *The Face* by William Wall: Fitzgerald's Park
3. *On Buxton Hill* by Kevin Barry: Sunday's Well
4. *Trees* by Mel O'Doherty: Greenmount
5. *A Love Letter in the Midsummer* by Danny Denton: Sullivan's Quay
6. *Gruffalo* by Jamie O'Connell: Cork City Centre
7. *Dog Collar* by Oonagh Montague: St Anne's Church
8. *The Face* by William Wall: Sidney Place
9. *Lost Property* by Mary Morrissy: The Elysian
10. *Gruffalo* by Jamie O'Connell: Old Blackrock Road
11. *Lost Property* by Mary Morrissy: Lichfield Cottage, Ballintemple

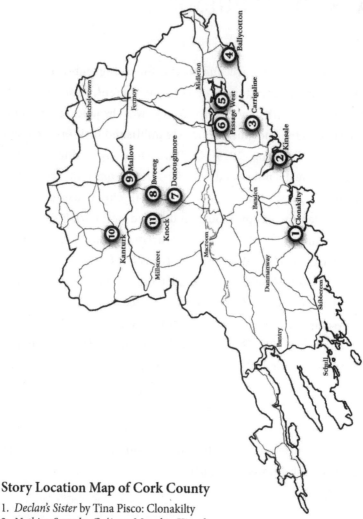

## Story Location Map of Cork County

1. *Declan's Sister* by Tina Pisco: Clonakilty
2. *Nothing Surer* by Gráinne Murphy: Kinsale
3. *Black Dog Running* by Sean Tanner: Carrigaline
4. *The Cook and the Star* by Anne O'Leary: Ballycotton
5. *Ciúnas* by Fiona Whyte: Passage West
6. *Noah Should Have Read Comics* by Marie Gethins: Passage West
7. *Along the Heron-Studded River* by Danielle McLaughlin: Donoughmore
8. *Where as a Child I'd Been* by Donal Moloney: Bweeng
9. *A Pure Dote* by Tadhg Coakley: Mallow
10. *His Shoes* by Eileen O'Donoghue: Kanturk
11. *Knock* by Martina Evans: Knock

# ACKNOWLEDGEMENTS

Acknowledgements are due to the following publications in which some of the stories, or versions thereof, first appeared: 'On Buxton Hill' by Kevin Barry was broadcast on RTÉ *Drama on One* and was previously published in *Winter Papers 1* (Curlew Editions, 2015); 'A Pure Dote' by Tadhg Coakley was previously published in *The First Sunday in September* (Mercier Press, 2018); 'A Love Letter in the Midsummer' by Danny Denton was previously published in the *Irish Examiner* on 2nd August, 2020; 'Knock' by Martina Evans was previously published in *The Windows of Graceland* (Carcanet Press, 2016); 'Noah Should Have Read Comics' by Marie Gethins won first prize in the Words on Water Festival 2019 short story competition and was previously published in *The Echo* on Thursday, 10th October, 2019; 'Along the Heron-Studded River' by Danielle McLaughlin was previously published in *Dinosaurs on Other Planets* (Stinging Fly, 2014); 'Trees' by Mel O'Doherty was previously published in Issue No 40 of *Southword Literary Journal*, 2021; and 'Declan's Sister' by Tina Pisco was previously published in *Sunrise Sunset and other fictions* (Fish Publishing, 2016).

# CONTRIBUTORS' NOTES

Kevin Barry is the author of four novels, including *The Heart in Winter* in 2024, and three story collections. He also works as a playwright and screenwriter and he co-edits and publishes the *Winter Papers* anthology. He lives in County Sligo.

Tadhg Coakley is the author of five books: *Before He Kills Again* (2023); *The Game: A Journey into the Heart of Sport* (2022), which was shortlisted as the Irish Sports Book of The Year; *Whatever It Takes* (2020), the 2020 Cork One City, One Book choice; *Everything* (2020), the autobiography of Denis Coughlan, which he co-wrote; and *The First Sunday in September* (2018). His short stories, articles and essays have been published in *The Stinging Fly, Winter Papers, The Irish Examiner, The Irish Times, The42.ie, Aethlon, The Holly Bough* and elsewhere.

Danny Denton is the author of the novels *The Earlie King & the Kid in Yellow* and *All Along The Echo*. He lectures on writing at University College Cork and is a contributing editor to *The Stinging Fly*.

Martina Evans is the author of thirteen books of poetry and prose. *American Mules* (Carcanet 2021) won the Pigott Poetry Prize in 2022 and was both a TLS and Sunday Independent Book of the Year. Her latest narrative poem, *The Coming Thing* was published in September 2023. She is an *Irish Times* books critic.

Marie Gethins featured in *Winter Papers*, Bristol Short Story Award, NFFD Anthologies, *Banshee, Fictive Dream, Pure Slush, Bath Flash Fiction Anthologies, FlashBack Fiction, Jellyfish*

*Review, Litro, The Cormorant Broadsheet, Australian Book Review* and others. She was awarded B.A.'s in English Literature and Dramatic Art/Dance from U.C. Berkeley, an MSt in Creative Writing from the University of Oxford and a PhD in Creative Writing from the University of Limerick. Selected for Best Microfictions, BIFFY50, Best Small Fictions, she edits for flash ezine *Splonk* and critiques for the Oxford Flash Fiction Prize.

Danielle McLaughlin's short story collection *Dinosaurs on Other Planets* was published in 2015 by The Stinging Fly Press. In 2019, she was a Windham-Campbell Prize recipient, and won the Sunday Times Audible Short Story Award. Her first novel, *The Art of Falling*, was published in 2021 by John Murray and was shortlisted for the Dublin Literary Award 2022. In 2023 she was a recipient of a Markievicz Award.

Donal Moloney is a freelance writer and translator. His short stories have appeared in *New Irish Writing* (Irish Times); *The Moth; Cork Words 2; Long Story, Short; Sharp Sticks, Driven Nails* (Stinging Fly); *Verge* (Monash University); *The Galway Review 4;* and *Boyne Berries*. He has also published several essays in the *Dublin Review of Books*. The recipient of an Arts Council of Ireland literature bursary, he lives in Cork City.

Oonagh Montague is a writer based in Cork. Her fiction has been published in *Winter Papers*. She is a former journalist and editor of Arts Ireland.

Mary Morrissy is the author of four novels, *Mother of Pearl, The Pretender, The Rising of Bella Casey* and most recently *Penelope Unbound*. She has also published two collections of stories,

A *Lazy Eye* and *Prosperity Drive* and has been anthologised widely. Her work has won her the Hennessy Prize and a Lannan Foundation Award. A member of Aosdána, she is a journalist, teacher of creative writing and a literary mentor. She blogs at marymorrissy.com.

Gráinne Murphy is a West Cork-based novelist and short story writer. She has published three novels with Legend Press: *Where the Edge Is* (2020), *The Ghostlights* (2021) and *Winter People* (2022), with a fourth novel, *Greener*, forthcoming in 2024. Her short story, 'Further West', was longlisted for the Sunday Times Audible Short Story Award in 2021, with other stories published in *Cork Words 3*, *The Holly Bough* and a Fish Anthology. 'Time Immemorial', an essay on grief and the quiet power of country graveyards, was published by *The Milk House* in April 2021 and nominated for that year's Pushcart Prize.

Jamie O'Connell is the author of the best-selling novel, *Diving for Pearls* (Doubleday UK). *Diving for Pearls* was runner-up for The Gordon Bowker Volcano Prize (The Society of Authors 2022) and shortlisted for The Sunday Independent Newcomer of the Year (The Irish Book Awards 2021).

Mel O'Doherty has been shortlisted for the Francis MacManus Award and the Seán Ó Faoláin International Short Story Award and longlisted for The Sunday Times Short Story Award. His stories have been published in a number of literary magazines and anthologies as well as in *The Irish Times* and broadcast on RTE Radio. His debut novel, *Fallen*, was published in 2021. He lives in Douglas, Cork with his wife and three children.

Eileen O'Donoghue is a Cork writer living in Kerry. Her short fiction has been longlisted for the Fabula Press prize in 2017, published in *The Quarryman* in 2017, 2018 and 2021; shortlisted for Fish in 2018; highly commended for the Bridport short story Prize in 2021; highly commended in the Michael Terence short story competition 2021; a finalist in the Screencraft 2023 cinematic short story competition and shortlisted for New Irish writing. *Blackwater,* her first novel, was highly commended at the Irish Writers Centre Novel Fair 2021 and shortlisted for the Bridport Peggy-Chapman Andrews first novel award in 2022.

Anne O'Leary won the Molly Keane Award 2018 and the From the Well Short Story Competition 2017; was runner-up in the Aurora Prize for Fiction 2023, Bournemouth Writing Prize 2021, Irish Novel Fair 2016 and 2021, and UCC/Carried in Waves Short Story Competition 2015; shortlisted for the ChipLitFest Short Story Award 2023 and Colm Tóibín International Short Story Award 2016 and 2017; and longlisted for the Caledonia Novel Award 2022 and Cambridge Short Story Prize 2020. Her work has been published in journals and anthologies in the UK and Ireland. She is a former Frank O'Connor mentorship bursary recipient.

Tina Pisco is a writer of novels, newspaper columns, poetry and short stories. In 2020/21 she became the first Writer-in-Residence for Cork City Libraries, and in 2021/22 was awarded the prestigious Frank O'Connor Fellowship by the Munster Literature Centre. Her first short story collection, *Sunrise Sunset and other fictions,* (Fish, 2016) was longlisted for the Edge Hill Prize.

Sean Tanner's fiction has appeared or is forthcoming in *The Irish Times, The Irish Independent, The Stinging Fly, The Lonely Crowd, The Forge Literary Magazine, The Moth Magazine, Litro Magazine* and *The London Magazine*, among others. In 2017 he won the Hennessy New Irish Writing Award for first fiction, and in 2018 he received the John McGahern Award for literature. In 2021 he was awarded a full literature bursary from the Arts Council of Ireland. His play *I Could Have Been a Dancer* has been shown in The New Theatre Dublin (2022) and The Set Theatre Kilkenny (2023).

William Wall is the author of seven novels, most recently *Empty Bed Blues* (New Island, 2023), six collections of poetry and three of short fiction. He has won or been shortlisted for many prizes and his work has been translated into many languages. More information at williamwall.net.

Fiona Whyte is a writer based in Crosshaven, County Cork. Her short fiction has appeared in *Cork Words 2, Dorothy Dunnett/Historical Writers' Association Anthology, Crannóg Magazine, Quarryman, The Holly Bough, The Echo, Long Story, Short and Brevity is the Soul: Wit From Lockdown Ireland*. She holds a PhD in Creative Writing from University College Cork and has been awarded funding by the Arts Council of Ireland, Cork County Council and the Irish Research Council. Her debut novel is forthcoming with Lightning Books in 2024. She is currently working on a second novel.